When she looke  watching her, buttoning his shirt over his blushed. Neither of them spoke.

They wandered among the trees toward home. White butterflies danced above the wild strawberries where the bees had been and the scent of skunk still lingered.

"You shouldn't come out here alone," Arthur said. "You can't be sure what you might see."

"Maybe you ought to wear a bathing suit." She glanced at him but he watched the path ahead. He didn't care that she'd seen him without his clothes on, she knew that.

"Where'd you get the welts?"

"Fell. Wrestling Ol' Pete."

He gently took her hand. Crickets chirruped. Sunlight brightened the woods' canopy as they neared the Lees' property line. He paused.

"I'll wait a while," he said, letting go of her hand. "You leave first."

She looked up. Why after so many years of thinking of him as a brother, as a pesky brother even, why suddenly did she feel so differently standing near him? She knew Gram was waiting. But she suddenly loathed the Wickhams and she couldn't tell anyone why.

She touched a top button on his shirt. His chest rose and fell with soft breaths. She tucked a strand of wet hair behind his ear. Their foreheads pressed together, his hair falling forward around their faces. Their noses touched. Then their lips. She dangled her arms at her sides so she wouldn't bump his sores.

Seneca Lake

by

Emily Heebner

Seneca Lake

Cover Art by *Kristian Norris*

The Wild Rose Press, Inc.
PO Box 708
Adams Basin, NY 14410-0708
Visit us at www.thewildrosepress.com

Publishing History
First Vintage Rose Edition, 2019
Print ISBN 978-1-5092-2657-3
Digital ISBN 978-1-5092-2658-0

Published in the United States of America

Dedication

For my mother, Polly Stevens Heebner

Chapter 1

Meg plucked off her apron, hung it on a hook, and dashed out the diner door just in time to see a bus vanish around the corner. She knew the driver's late run of the day, having ridden it many times. The bus would clump along Main Street past the billboard of a tilting ocean liner with words that warned "Loose Lips Might Sink Ships." Then the driver would shift into low gear for the steep climb up Seneca Lake's east shore.

"Darn."

Meg kicked the pebbles along the dirt path next to the highway. It would be such a long wait at the bus stop now. She was sure she'd miss her ride to the County Fair with Hank Wickham. She lifted her pigtails onto the top of her head and held them there with one hand while she walked. Sweat drew the collar of her white uniform to her neck. Insects droned while poplar trees fluttered their leaves. Up ahead where the road curved with the shore, asphalt shimmered like a mirage in a Hollywood movie.

If only the Dewitts hadn't ordered four banana splits after their steaks with fries, Meg probably could've caught her bus. She could just see Gram shake her head and say, "It's not good to be late for things all the time, honey."

Meg pictured Hank Wickham, with his sky blue eyes, handsome in his Army uniform, leaning over the cash register, offering her a ride to Horseheads tonight. Tan, tall, and suddenly so friendly, he'd smelled of cologne. He seemed different since his training in Oklahoma. Had he stopped by on purpose just to see her? Had he and Jenny Mae broken up? Meg couldn't imagine why he would break up with the prettiest girl in Watkins and then pay attention to her, Meg, the sixteen-year-old smart kid with freckles who'd skipped eighth grade. But maybe her best friend Greta Lee was right. Maybe Meg really had gotten better looking this summer. Something must have changed.

In a couple of days, Hank Wickham would ship out from Camp Shanks. More and more boys from Watkins had been heading off to war. Meg whispered a prayer for Hank and the other boys, and for her brother Ron, too, of course. *Please bring them home safe.*

Passing the old red brick mortuary on the way to the bus stop, Meg stared straight ahead, trying to ignore the picture that always flashed into her mind. Every time she walked to the bus stop, the memory gnawed at her, never letting her go, as if it had happened just yesterday. But she must have been only two or three at the time. She couldn't understand why she remembered it so clearly, being held up by Gram and looking down into Great Aunt May's casket. She could still feel Gram's sturdy arms around her as she looked down and saw Aunt May's stiff leather skin pulled tight against her skull.

One day Gram would explain everything, Meg knew. Then she'd learn why she'd been sent as a baby first to live with her Aunt May, and then with Gram and Gramps after Aunt May died. Gram and Gramps lived above the Valois Saloon, across the street from Meg's own parents, across the street even from her own sisters and only brother, Ron. Meg always wondered why she'd never lived with her own mother and daddy. But Gram never offered to explain why. And Meg was afraid to ask.

Suddenly a rusted pickup truck pulled onto the shoulder of the road up ahead. Meg could see Arthur's braid through the window of his truck's cab. His Seneca features reflected in his sideview mirror as she trotted toward him.

"Need a lift?" he called back over his shoulder.

"Sure, thanks!" Meg ran up to the passenger side and yanked open the door.

Arthur was dusting the passenger seat, then wiped his hand on his overalls and reached across the seat to help Meg hoist herself up. She noticed his T-shirt was damp under his arm but the palm of his hand was dry. His muscle bulged like Popeye's as he pulled her up. She felt shy all of a sudden after she shut the door to the cab, being alone with him. But why? She'd taken plenty of rides from him before. Arthur was like a brother. She'd known him most of her life.

"Sorry about the dirt." Arthur glanced in the rearview mirror as he veered the truck with a bump onto the highway. He shot a grin at Meg, his teeth white against sunburnt lips.

"How's Ol' Pete?" Meg asked, guessing from the smell of the truck that Arthur had delivered the Lee's hog to the livestock competition at the County Fair.

"He's bound to take blue, or I'll feed my ponytail to the beast who does." He snipped the air with two fingers. "I got a good feeling we'll make Greta's Daddy proud. Ol' Pete knows he's prettier than the rest. If he don't snort and stick his nose in the air like some beauty queen every time folks come around! Best hog I ever knew." He smiled over at Meg, then looked back at the road. "Greta took blue for her boysenberry pie."

"Oh, good," Meg said, inhaling the odor of the cab, a mixture of gasoline fumes, manure, and day-old sweat. She liked Arthur for how hard he worked on Greta's parents' farm, even while he struggled to finish school. She wondered if the reason he'd been held back a grade was that he'd been busy instead of just dumb. She never liked how the other girls laughed about his smell on days he milked heifers. She had a talent for tolerating bad smells selectively—she enjoyed her daddy's cigarette smoke but anyone else's made her cough. Daddy's smoke meant his gravel voice asking "what's new," his grease-stained hands holding a stray cat. Arthur's truck smell meant county fairs and carnival barkers, Greta's 4-H pies, strings of sparkly lights at dances under the tents on summer nights. Meg again pictured Hank Wickham, so strong now from training at Fort Sill. She hoped Hank would ask her to dance tonight.

"Goin' to the fair?" Arthur called over the rush of wind from the open windows.

"I want to. Probably missed my ride, though."

"I can take ya." Arthur nodded for emphasis as they careened up the two-laned New York State highway.

"Oh, thanks."

Meg hoped she could hitch a ride home from the fair with Hank Wickham in his father's Ford. At least now she'd have time to clean up properly and rid herself of the smell of catsup and cleanser. She leaned her head back against the seat. Knowing Arthur and his late afternoon chores, she could probably pin-curl her hair and even have time for the curls to set.

Yellow seams of late afternoon light streaked across Seneca Lake. Shadows from trees flickered on and off like shutters in the truck cab. Cooler air gusted in through the open windows. Arthur drove fast but not crazy. He didn't show off like other boys.

The Baptist church bells rang six times as Arthur parked his truck beside Meg's parents' stoop. Meg could see her daddy through the front window, rocking his rocker, cigarette stub poised between two fingers. He waved to her. She waved back. A gray cat nibbled table scraps from a tea saucer at the bottom of the stoop.

"Hi, Daddy!" she called.

"Half hour?" Arthur asked.

Meg nodded.

"You gonna be here or at your gram's?" Arthur tipped his head in the direction of the Valois Saloon across the highway.

"At Gram's." Meg spoke quietly as she let herself down out of the truck. "She's got the shower." Both Meg and Arthur smiled. Everyone knew her parents owned the only house in Valois that still lacked indoor plumbing.

Arthur studied her for a moment, then jerked his head away to check for traffic. "Be back." He pulled onto the empty highway to drive half a block to the Lee residence. Meg crossed the highway, turning back to wave to her daddy and to watch Arthur's truck crawl up the Lee driveway past forsythia and lilac bushes. Then the truck disappeared around the back of the main house in the direction of the guest house where Arthur lived with his grandmother, the Lees' maid.

Meg thought of her best friend Greta, born a Lee with all the money in the world, spending the whole day today at the county fair. Sometimes Meg couldn't help envying girls who didn't need to work. Still, Meg was grateful for her job at the diner. She pictured her sisters working like men at the army depot, Viv and June loading heavy crates at the hot warehouse. Meg felt sorry for them. She knew she was lucky that her friends could drop by the diner for coffee and pie during her shifts. And she jiggled the change in her pocket. This'd make enough to buy the new saddle shoes she'd been saving up for all summer.

Inside the Valois Saloon, Meg held her breath against the stench of beer and stale cigars as she sidled along the edge of the room. She heard Brandy, the pregnant Labrador Retriever, thump her tail on the oak floor.

"That Arthur dropped you off?" Charley, Brandy's owner, the slight but pot-bellied bartender, called from behind the bar.

"Missed my bus," Meg said.

"Hank Wickham says to tell you he's sorry he missed you. Had to get to Horseheads for the truck pull."

"Okay. Thanks." Privacy never did exist in Valois. She tried to hurry up the back staircase.

"Be careful driving around with Arthur, Megs. His daddy died in a car crash, you know. Them injuns can't drink."

At the top of the landing, Meg pushed the door open into a bright, white-walled flat that overlooked the lake. An elderly Siamese padded toward her. Meg reached low to scratch behind the deaf feline's ears, but Sam rolled onto her side, as if trying to show her belly. Meg stooped to pat the silver-gray tummy and was thanked with motoring purrs.

"Hey, Sam," she whispered.

Gram looked up from her embroidery, her rocker creaking as she tipped back. Gramps grunted from his chair, a throne of crocheted throws, colorful magnets for cat hair and axle grease.

"Goin' to the dance?" Gramps shook his newspaper and frowned.

"Well, I guess I missed my ride with Hank Wickham, but maybe he'll bring me home after." Meg tried to disappear down the hallway to her room. "Guess I better wash up."

"How you plannin' to get there now?" Gram's tone stopped Meg and made her turn. "Who's drivin'?"

"Arthur'll take me," Meg said softly.

Her grandparents shot looks at each other, the way they did whenever Meg wanted to do something she knew they were sure to disapprove of.

"Hold there, young lady." Gramps rubbed his eyes. "I'm not too keen on you drivin' all the way to Horseheads in that truck of his. Got nothin' against Arthur hisself, you understand."

Gram seemed to focus on Meg's impatient hand-me-down shoes.

"What if your Gramps drives you?" Gram suggested.

"Sure, I'll take you, Meggie. How 'bout it?"

Meg felt her face burn. Why did everyone blame Arthur for things he never did? Didn't he take care of his grandmother and work hard on the Lees' farm? Sometimes Meg thought he showed more responsibility than just about all the other boys, even Hank Wickham.

"Arthur's a good driver, Gram. Better than just about everybody."

Her grandparents shot looks at each other again.

"We just want you safe, honey, is all." Gram patted her gray knotted braid at the nape of her neck. "Best get washed. When's Arthur want to leave?"

Meg was already half way down the hall when she called out, "Half hour!"

****

A sunset of feathered orange and violet strands lit the drive to the fair. Meg's curls tickled her with the rush of wind through the truck window. She closed her eyes. Arthur had swept the truck out and strewn lilac branches along the dash. Meg smiled at the absence of Ol' Pete's stink.

"Goin' to the dance?" Arthur unbuttoned the cuff of his white collared shirt and rolled up a sleeve as he drove.

"Sure."

Meg hoped Arthur wouldn't ask her to dance tonight. She wanted to dance with Hank Wickham and worried Hank might get the wrong impression if he learned that Arthur had brought her. She liked Arthur as a friend, but that was all.

Arthur rolled up his other sleeve, then arched his arm on top of his head and yawned. "I been up since four." He grinned. "But don't worry, I'll get ya there safe. Promise." He was slumped in his seat, steering with one hand.

"Would it help if we sing?" Meg had learned this

trick from Gram when Gramps would get sleepy at the wheel at night.

"All right, but be loud," Arthur warned her. "I don't sing so good myself."

Meg led off with a medley from *Oklahoma*. She and Greta had memorized the Broadway album, thanks to the Lee family phonograph. And Arthur had picked up the melodies when he worked in the yard just outside the living room window. He punched the words with spirit.

They sped past miles of well-groomed cornfields. At a fork in the road, the sign for Horseheads appeared. On either side of it, two red wooden poles displayed horse skulls. Arthur glanced at Meg, then drove in the direction of the fair grounds.

"What was that?" Meg asked.

"Mr. Wickham's running the committee this year. Guess folks like to remember how Horseheads got its name."

Meg knew the Revolutionary War story of how George Washington had ordered all Seneca villages in the Finger Lakes destroyed. She'd seen the reenactments a couple of times with Mr. Wickham dressed like James Clinton of the infamous Sullivan-Clinton Campaign.

"Where on earth did he get those skulls?" Meg asked.

"My guess is they come from Rochester. The museum up there, that's where Arthur Parker collects Seneca stuff. He's part Seneca himself, see. My mother used to take me and my grandma there when I was little. I remember horse skulls on sticks, behind glass."

"It's so gory," Meg said. "Those poor horses."

"Yep, that son-of-a-gun Sullivan wore his horses out. Just left them dead, lying everywhere. Makes me sick just to picture it. The Senecas came back when it was safe, finally, and put their heads on the poles. So's to set their spirits free."

Meg turned to watch the horse skulls in the distance. She wondered what Hank Wickham thought of this eerie memorial.

****

Friday night at the 102nd annual Chemung County Fair was in full swing when Arthur pulled his truck off the paved road. Every variety of pickup truck was represented, parked in makeshift rows on the fallow cornfields surrounding the fair grounds.

"Like to hop out?" Arthur shifted into neutral near the entrance.

"Sure." Meg blushed, trying to control her skirt while she slid out of the cab. When she turned back to close the door, Arthur's eyes were set on his rearview mirror. "Thanks," she told him. Arthur nodded and headed off toward the fields.

Early evening sent a soft breeze through Meg's peach cotton shirtwaist. June bugs crashed and sizzled against the twinkle lights on a ticket bower near the fair entrance. Meg wandered along the edge of the crowd toward the exhibition tents.

4-H displays were always easy to find. Quilts of stitched-together cotton yo-yo's hung in a horseshoe-shape around the entrance to the tent. Twinkle lights lit up the inside. Tables crowded with homemade dresses, quilts, and baked goods testified to a wealth of local talent. Meg found Greta's mother seated at the far end of the tent.

"Evening, Miz Lee. Have you seen Greta?" Meg gave a slight curtsy whenever she greeted Mrs. Lee. She was almost as fond of Greta's mom as she was of Greta herself.

"Over to the truck pull, Meg, if it's still goin'. After that, try the dance. South end near the popcorn stand, she said to tell you. I like your dress. Peach becomes you."

"Think so?"

Meg tried not to giggle or squirm. Or run her hands all over herself in embarrassment. She was trying to learn to accept compliments. Her brother Ron had given her a sit-down talk that last time he was home on leave. "You got to smile when people say nice things," he'd said. "And not argue with them and tell them they're wrong."

Meg thanked Mrs. Lee properly and set off in the direction of the tractor pull. Luckily Greta's strawberry curls would be easy to spot in a crowd. A loudspeaker announced the final tractor competition of the day.

"Bo Grimsby will challenge our champion, Hank Wickham!"

Barkers called to Meg as she ran past them. She could hear the crowd cheer. She slid through a mass of men drinking beer till she could see the portable stands. She scanned quickly for Greta's hair, then set her eyes on Hank. He stood tall on his tractor in the center of the field. Hank and his brand-new emerald green John Deere. He waved in a grand manner in Meg's direction. She almost waved back, then remembered he needed glasses, even though he seldom wore them. She'd seen him wear them in the library, before he enlisted. He was "one of Watkins' brightest"—that's what everyone said about Hank.

"All right, gents," the announcer called. "Start your engines. Sled riders, get ready."

A gunshot rang out. Both sets of tractor wheels rolled, kicking up mud behind them. Several men and boys in overalls jumped onto the backs of sleds attached to the tractors. Bo Grimsby's machine began to smoke and slow down. Hank's John Deere continued strong.

The crowd chanted, "Hank, Hank, Hank…"

But Meg noticed the Wickham cousin from Pennsylvania on the back of Hank's sled. He was clutching his leg in an odd, contorted angle. Meg got the feeling he was about to fall. The crowd kept on cheering.

Both tractors slogged toward the finish line, slowed by the drag of mud and weight on the sleds. Hank waved his fingers at the portable stands in a "V for victory" sign. Meg wished he would turn and see that his cousin was hurt.

Hank shifted into a lower gear, ready to make a final dash for the finish line. When the tractor jerked, Hank's cousin fell backward off the sled into the mud. He screamed. Blood spread down the leg of his uniform.

The crowd hushed.

Bo Grimsby yanked his tractor into reverse, just missing the cousin's head by a few inches. A group of men charged out from the stands onto the field. Meg spotted a black ponytail on one of the men, just as people stood up in front of her and blocked her view.

Chapter 2

An hour later, Meg and Greta stood outside the main entrance to the dance tent. June bugs harassed them. Inside, couples of all ages twirled and promenaded to a caller's bidding in time with a fiddler's jig. Meg loved to square dance. But she knew Hank wouldn't get back from Schuyler County tonight. He'd be waiting at the hospital for his cousin's leg to get fixed. Then he'd need to drive him home in the Wickham Ford.

"Why couldn't they use Chemung Hospital? It's closer," Meg asked Greta.

"They say the boy's staying in Ithaca with his grandparents. I overheard it in the ladies' room."

The banjo player's final strum signaled the dancers to bow and curtsy. Then the band laid down its instruments to take a break. A mass of colorful skirts dispersed, jostling in a mayhem of searches for refreshments or new partners.

"Come on," Greta said, nudging Meg.

They sidled along the inside edge of the tent toward the punch table. Kerosene lamps cast a rosy luster on the bare arms and flushed cheeks they passed. Clusters of balloons glowed translucent like butterfly wings. Sweat heated the air laced with women's fragrance and pipe tobacco.

"Meg! Greh-ta!" Anne Becker called to the girls

from behind a cut-glass punch bowl. A jolly British woman of thirty, she ladled raspberry Kool-Aid into cups her husband handed to thirsty dancers.

The skirts of Meg and Greta's shirtwaists flitted against their legs as they rushed over.

"Hi ya, Mrs. B! Hi, Mr. B!"

"Punch, girls?" Mr. B flashed his grin. His blond mustache and beard framed large teeth, and his cheeks shone like a young Santa impersonator's.

"Sure, thanks, Mr. B. Oh, Mrs. B! Did you hear what happened?" Greta flattened her hands on the table and pressed her hips against the edge to claim a spot between some of the dancers. She recounted every detail of the tractor pull debacle.

The Beckers were English teachers at Watkins Glen High School who read poetry together and longed to have a baby but hadn't had any luck yet. Meg and Greta had just finished junior English with Mrs. B and would have Mr. B for senior English in the fall. Mrs. B, who stood a full two inches taller than her husband, rarely wore high heels.

"Yes, yes, I heard some of that," Mrs. B said. "I bet it's left a girl or two disappointed tonight." Meg didn't miss the twinkle in her eye.

"Sure hope that busted leg'll be all right," said Mr. B.

"Aw, I think it'll be all right." Meg recognized Arthur's voice from behind her. He swept around to take the cup Mr. B held out especially for him. His white shirtsleeve had spots of mud and blood.

"Did you see the leg?" Mr. B asked. Arthur nodded.

"Arthur made a stretcher for him," Meg said.

"Helped get him into the Ford, too."

"Then you'd have a firm opinion on that break, wouldn't you, Arthur?" Mr. B said.

Most folks knew Arthur had a knack for setting the broken legs of young calves. He could do it as well as any vet in Schuyler County. But few adults ever bothered to compliment him for it.

"I understood that boy was an athlete," Mr. B said. "Glad to know he can recover. But it may keep him out of the war. I bet Hank feels bad about that."

"You girls going to dance?" Mrs. B asked.

Greta leaned forward, as if trying not to be overheard by the others. "Who with?" Greta fanned her hand at the crowd. "They're either too young or way too old!"

Dancers set their empty cups on the table and circulated back toward the dance area. Tiny puddles formed in the dirt from spills.

Greta sighed loudly. "High school boys are so immature."

The Beckers and Meg glanced at Arthur, who pretended to be interested in the band gathering for its next set.

"Sorry, Arthur," Greta said. Arthur turned with a surprised look, then he laughed. The Beckers and Meg laughed, too. "All right, well, anyway." Greta blushed. "I just can't wait for college, let me tell you."

Meg felt lucky. She still liked boys who were seventeen or eighteen. But Greta was a year older than Meg. She couldn't be bothered with boys younger than twenty. And most of them were off at war.

"How about you, Meg?" Mrs. B said, narrowing her eyes. "Looking forward to college?"

Meg blushed and looked away. "Don't really know how I could." She sensed Arthur's eyes on her, as well as Mr. B's. At five foot five, Mr. B could talk to Meg at eye level.

"Well, Meg, I've heard about those grades of yours," he said. "You could go just about anywhere." Meg glanced over at Arthur, who was looking at the ground.

"Yeah." Greta laughed. "I wish I had Meg's grades. So does my mother!"

Meg spotted her big sisters, June and Viv, standing close by with friends and cousins. Meg's parents had disappointed June recently when they told her they couldn't afford to send her to nursing school in the fall after all. Sure, Daddy's gas pump did a lot better now since the war started, but he most likely couldn't help his daughters go to college any time soon. And Meg didn't want to hurt him by asking and setting him up to have to say no.

"I'll be all right without college," Meg said, swilling some punch and setting the cup on the table. "We better get dance partners before we miss out."

As soon as she'd said it, she wished she hadn't. Oh, why couldn't she listen to Gram and think before she let things fly out of her mouth? Meg avoided Arthur's eyes and watched her sisters whisper and nod in her direction. They knew, no doubt, that Hank had asked her to ride over with him and that she'd ended up riding in Arthur's truck. And if they saw her dancing with Arthur, she'd never hear the end of it. "Why do you always embarrass us?" they'd say. Meg sensed Arthur close to her, his earthen smell, the combination of sawdust and dried grass. He was eyeing the band with a furrowed brow, his hands planted on his hips.

"I guess I could be your partner," he said softly.

Meg bit inside her lower lip and watched the caller drink down his glass of punch. She wondered how she could be smart in school but dumb in life.

"All right, Greta," Mrs. B announced. "I give my husband permission to dance with you."

Greta jumped and clapped her hands. Mrs. B pushed Mr. B out from behind the punch table. He darted her a good-humored but defiant look. She smiled back, as if she might reward him later.

"Just send him back in one piece, please."

Greta grabbed Mr. B's hand and dragged him toward a circle that was forming with other teachers from Watkins.

Meg's sisters partnered with distant cousins who worked at the Army depot, one with flat feet and the other with crossed eyes.

"Well?" Arthur let out a sigh. Kool-Aid lingered on his breath.

Meg re-tied her shoe to stall for time. When she stood up again, she noticed his shirt was tucked neatly into the waist of his blue jeans. His rolled-up sleeves showed his taut arms. The lights in the tent made his skin maroon.

The fiddler plucked and tuned his strings, then raced through Irish scales. The dance was about to begin. Meg sensed Mrs. B's scrutiny.

What was so bad about dancing with Arthur, anyway? And why did people care what she did? Were their lives that boring? She surrendered and tugged Arthur's sleeve.

"Okay," she said, and began to walk toward

Greta's circle, conscious of her sisters' stares.

"I never done…" Arthur confessed down into Meg's ear as he followed behind her. She turned, but continued to walk. She felt her skirt swish against his leg. He leaned his head down closer to her, his mouth curved downward.

"I never done it."

For a moment she thought they should retreat and save face. What if he fell, or tripped? Or let go her hand? But the bustle of bodies and tuning instruments stirred her. She loved to dance.

"Don't worry, it's not a test."

She glanced up just in time to see his wince. Was she heaven-bent on tormenting him? Just like Gram said, "Oh, Meg, sometimes you say the meanest things." She tried to fix it.

"Don't be scared, Arthur. I'll help you."

They arrived at Greta's circle.

"Oh, good," Mr. B said. "Now we're set."

Meg and Arthur nodded to Greta, then acknowledged the others, who smiled and murmured, "How-do."

Their dancing comrades included former teachers of Meg's—Mr. Jones, the calculus teacher, a heavy smoker, and his wife, the home ec mistress, who excelled in sewing crazy quilts; Miss Charbeau, the biology teacher whose long blonde curls framed a sweet face; and Mr. Dunne, nearly sixty, the music teacher who had the energy of three people.

"Meg! Arthur!" Mr. Dunne announced in a tenor that Meg felt sure everyone in the tent could hear. "Glad to see you."

Arthur's pinched nose meant the organs in his body

were twisting into rubber spirals. Meg poked his sleeve.

"Uh, thank you, sir." Arthur coughed.

"Now look out, everyone," Miss Charbeau declared. "Mr. Dunne's won some contests in his day. We're all about to learn a thing or two!"

The fiddler began, and the band joined in: a spirited banjo, a double bass, and a tambourine. All the men in the circle bowed to the women's curtsies, but Arthur's bows possessed a natural grace.

"Palm up," Meg told him, anticipating the next step. "Put your palm up." She held hers down and reached for his hand.

"Circle left!" the caller sang.

Meg nudged Arthur to the left and around they went with the others in time to the music. Concentration replaced the worry in his eyes, and his palm was warm.

"Circle right!" All the dancers in the tent reversed.

"Forward and back!"

"Four!" Meg flashed four fingers. They took four steps forward and four steps back.

"Balance and swing!"

Arthur stopped and stared. Meg clamped his right hand onto her waist and grabbed his left hand. She held her breath, but before she could lead, he was swinging her. Her skirt and hair flew. His ponytail swung out. When the music slowed, he slowed down too. In control, he returned her to her spot. But she wasn't dizzy. Their eyes had been locked.

"I thought you'd never done this before," she panted.

"I didn't."

"Promenade."

Arthur mimicked Mr. Dunne, who was sweeping

his arm around Miss Charbeau. Meg grinned as she hooked her hand on Arthur's shoulder.

"You two look like professionals," Mr. B called from across the circle. Meg and Arthur giggled, pausing to watch Mr. B and Greta tussle to untangle Greta's arm.

"Help us, Mr. Dunne!" Greta cried. "Please?"

"Stand tall, Greta," Mr. Dunne instructed. "See Miss Charbeau? Such lovely posture!" Mr. Dunne straightened himself. "Hold her firm, Ben," he said when it was time to swing. "Ben Becker. Hold her like Arthur does, or that poor girl's like to fly across the room!"

The pressure Arthur put on Meg's shoulder allowed her to abandon herself to their swing. She felt as if the fiddler played just for her. The room swirled into a blur of colorful skirts and light and loosened hair. When Arthur slowed down and restored her to her spot, she was barely dizzy.

"Allemande Left!"

Meg reached for Mr. Dunne's arm to draw herself past. "Fun, huh, Meg?"

Mr. B winked when he passed.

Mr. Jones nodded with patience, though his sleeve was drenched and sweat dripped off his jowls. She hoped he wouldn't collapse.

Arthur's arms welcomed her back and guided her about in a twirl.

"Do-si-do. Balance and swing!"

Arthur swung her faster. She closed her eyes and let her head fall back. This was better than a merry-go-round, better than skating. Arthur's firm grip fought the centrifugal force that tried to wrench her away. She wished she could spin forever.

"Ladies and gents, may I introduce the band?" the caller said when the set ended.

Catching her breath, Meg whispered to Arthur. "This next dance'll be the last. It's a waltz. Think down-up-up, down. It's easy."

Arthur slumped.

"Don't worry," she said. "You're a great dancer." His brown eyes stared, then they both laughed. His breath reminded her of weeds in bloom. Purple thistles and Queen Anne's Lace.

The fiddler made an announcement. "Let's thank our host, Reverend Silas MacFarlane from Elmira!" Everyone cheered as the caller took a bow and stepped off the platform. Then the fiddler nodded three times to the band and the final waltz commenced.

Arthur threw up his hands after two bad starts.

"Don't quit now," she told him. "Tell your feet what to do." She exaggerated the rhythm till Arthur caught on. "Look over there," she giggled. Arthur glanced across the circle.

Mr. Dunne and Miss Charbeau were waltzing near the most challenged dancer in the group, Mr. B, who was trampling Greta's feet.

Arthur's long legs took Meg clear across the tent. She wished he would keep his steps smaller, so as not to attract attention. Maybe his nervousness made him stride so far. She felt her sisters watching, so she focused instead on the expression on Arthur's face. She'd seen it before when he mended fixtures at the barn. Now he'd figured out how to swoop her and turn, so he watched the floor for open spaces while she watched his face.

****

When the music ended, Arthur spun Meg one last time. She lifted her hair off the back of her neck, looked him in the eye and announced, "I'm thirsty, all of a sudden!"

"Me, too." He beamed and stood tall to guide her toward the punch table, but they had to pass her sisters along the way.

"How you getting home, Meg?" Viv asked.

"Mrs. Lee, I think."

Greta and her mother waited with the Beckers. Mr. B was barefoot. Mrs. B and the Lee women were laughing.

"You dance nicely, Arthur," Mrs. Lee said.

"Thank you, ma'am."

"My husband told me you'd be staying the night with Ol' Pete. So I'll take the girls."

"I can bring Pete home tomorrow morning," Arthur said. "If that's all right. After they give out ribbons."

"Fine. I hope he wins. Mr. Lee phoned today from Rochester. Seems he's always on a trip when Pete's up for something. Mr. Lee's got his heart set on a blue ribbon. Shine Pete up real good, if you would."

"Yes, ma'am."

Meg and Greta said their goodnights to the Beckers and followed Mrs. Lee out of the tent, with Arthur trailing close behind them. Outside, the air felt almost chilly.

"Hey, Arthur!"

Meg peered in the direction of a boy's voice she knew, waiting for her eyes to adjust to the dark. Hank Wickham's younger brother, Al, stood slouched with a group of boys who would be juniors in the fall.

"Hey, Fred Astaire," said a friend of Al's whom Meg didn't like. He walked over and shook Arthur's hand. "So that's why they keep you out of the war. Got to keep our dancin' men away from them Nazis!" Two more of Al's friends slapped Arthur on the back, but Arthur didn't smile.

Al and his friends were seventeen, two years younger than Arthur, who was their classmate.

"Come, girls," Mrs. Lee said. She began to walk away from the tent.

"G'night, Arthur," Meg said. Arthur didn't respond.

"Meg." Mrs. Lee looped elbows with both girls to lead them out of the fair grounds. "Mrs. B spoke to me. What's this about you not going to college?"

Meg shot one look behind her and saw Al Wickham's friends laughing, steering Arthur in the direction of the beer tent.

Chapter 3

It was the middle of the night when Meg saw Arthur dash across the Lees' side lawn and disappear into the woods. His unbuttoned shirt flapped like wings behind him. His hair was loose. Meg ran barefoot on the silent highway. She called to him in a hoarse whisper, "Arthur!" He didn't look back.

She followed him into the thicket, tracking sounds of sticks breaking under his feet, leading toward the gully, to the black swimming hole at the foot of the waterfall, deep, deep in the woods. Tips of leaves touched Meg's cheeks. She clutched her thin gown to avoid snags on the brush.

The moon lit silver pathways between the shadows. Meg's legs were now a deer's legs. Her hooves crushed fragrance from pine needles to the rhythm of Arthur's chanted breaths.

Meg sat up with a start. Sunshine was pummeling her room and the alarm clock on the side table claimed ten past ten. She tossed off her blanket, peeling damp hair off her cheek, and took a sip of water from the glass Gram had left her.

Arthur's grandmother had once said, "In the days of Handsome Lake, people listened to their dreams. A dream will tell you who you are."

"That's witchcraft," Meg's sisters had said. "Don't turn pagan, or we'll have to tell Mom."

"You finally awake?" Gram called from the front room.

"Yes'm!" Meg paid a quick visit to the bathroom, then hurried back down the hall and poked her head into the front room, clutching the bodice of her nightgown. Samantha purred in the shadow of Gram's rocker near an open window.

"Come see me, honey," Gram said. "Your Gramps went to the baptism. Hand me that tumbler." She rocked forward to set her mending aside and to reach for a glass pitcher of lemonade with droplets running down its side. Ice cubes tinkled into Meg's glass. A handmade doily sported a circle of sweat which Gram covered when she set the pitcher down again. Meg sank back into the upholstery and draped a crocheted throw over her chest.

"Hank Wickham came by on his way to church this morning," Gram said. "You were out so late, I didn't want to wake you."

Gram discouraged Meg from going to church whenever she could. She didn't mind her playing piano alongside Greta, who played the organ. But Gram didn't like the reverend or the doctrine or the dunkings.

"Them wedding vows rile me 'specially," Gram would say. "A wife's to obey her husband like a servant? Who made up such nonsense!"

"Who's getting dunked today?" Meg sucked an ice cube, enjoying the fact that her sisters had probably heard about Hank's early morning sojourn over to the saloon.

"Charley's sister, I think. Seems she's sober since she found religion. Hope it's true. Hope it's not Reverend working her that other way he does."

"Gram."

"Well, you know how I feel. Just be careful over there."

"I am."

Although Meg listened, she found herself revisiting her dream. The silver moonlight. The rhythm of bare feet. The far-off sound of falling water. She tried harder to concentrate on Gram's blue eyes.

"Hank said he was sorry he missed you last night. Said he'll be by again later." Gram resumed her mending. "What do you think of that?"

"Hm?" Meg couldn't help but be flattered, though she pretended she wasn't. Oh, poor big sis Viv would be dying with envy. "Is the cousin all right?"

"Leg's broke. I never did understand why the men have to... Well, anyway." Gram rocked in her rocker. "Do you like Hank Wickham, honey?"

"Course. He got voted most popular his senior year. Can't believe he's calling on me."

"He sure looks fine in that uniform—Mm-hm."

Meg swallowed a last bit of lemonade and tried to picture Hank as he'd stood on his tractor. But her mind kept switching to Arthur's open shirt from her dream.

"Hank comes from a good family," Gram said. "It's time to consider such things." Meg tapped on her empty glass. "There ain't nothin' to be scared of if a boy calls on you proper like Hank does."

"I'm not scared of boys."

"Well, you should be."

Meg blushed. Gram stopped rocking and paused to choose her words more carefully.

"I don't mean that exactly, honey. But a young man like Hank, why, he'd listen if you said you wasn't ready for something. If he did something and you wasn't comfortable. He's brought up good. Other boys don't know such things. They might not listen."

Meg almost said, "You mean, like Arthur?" but she didn't. It made her mad that people assumed Arthur was rude or rough with girls. Whenever dogs or horses at the Lees' barn got frisky, Meg and Greta watched everything. They studied. Arthur disappeared.

"Don't worry. Ron told me what to do."

"He did?" Gram poised her needle in the air and held her mending against her belly. "Well?"

"I'd rather not repeat it."

"You're awful young," her brother had warned her when she started high school. "You'll be around older guys now. And sometimes you act older than you are. If things heat up and the guy won't stop, just kick 'em. You know, where it hurts."

"Well, if you like Hank, honey, I think it's fine," Gram said. "Seems he'd like to see you before he ships out."

Meg's stomach grumbled.

"Fix a sandwich. There's ham and one of my cucumbers. They come up mighty big this year."

From Gram's kitchen window Meg could see the crowd for the baptism gathering down the hill to the west, along the lake shore. She tried to pick out Hank, but couldn't. Then she looked at the Lees' property up the hill to the east and searched the lawn's edge where it adjoined the woods. A buzz of insects accompanied a stillness in the air, interrupted only by an occasional car passing on the highway. Meg dawdled, spreading mustard in parallel lines on her slice of ham, nibbling the crust off her slices of bread. She munched her cucumber like a crisp banana, eating the sandwich in separate pieces, watching the Lee place for Arthur.

"Guess I need a walk," she told Gram on her way to her bedroom to put on some clothes.

"What about Hank?" Gram looked up.

Meg turned and smiled. She didn't want to seem crabby. "I'll come right back. Slept too long. Got stiff."

She almost added, "Probably all that dancing last night," but she didn't.

Humidity weighted the air outside. Meg walked fast, hopeful that if she kept her head down her daddy might not look up from petting one of his stray cats or tipping the ash off his cigarette. Singing erupted from the baptism down the hill. She scuttled past the church and hurried across the highway. No cars were in view. She skirted around the front of the Lees' house and ran back to the barn.

Inside, manure and hay baked in the summer heat. A horse snorted. Ol' Pete snored in a lower stall. Meg wondered if Arthur slept hidden in a stall or overhead in the loft. But she didn't call his name. It felt strange to be alone in the barn today. The Lees would be at the baptism. She slipped back outside and headed for the woods.

The canopy of trees fluttered over the sounds of running water in the gully. Meg took off her hand-me-down slip-ons and stepped with care on the forest floor. Fallen needles pricked her arches at times, so she looked for smooth stones to tread on, or moss. Bees hummed near low patches of wild strawberries.

Meg listened to a tune in her head from *Oklahoma*, the one about a girl who knew right from wrong since the age of ten. She and Arthur had sung it in the truck.

Squirrels scampered up tree trunks onto bowing branches, almost in time to the rhythm of the song.

Then that line from *Oldtown Folks,* Mrs. Stowe's book, nagged at her. That part about "men that women are always wrecking themselves on." Why had Mrs. B recommended it especially to her for summer reading? That part about men that "make bewitching lovers, but terrible husbands." Was Hank Wickham that kind? She passed through a remnant smell of skunk.

Meg's mother had chosen an auto mechanic for her husband, a kind man with a sixth grade education. Gram had raised Daddy and Aunt Lizzie to be loyal and hard-working. But Meg's mother liked books and music. She'd been the first in her family to finish high school and get teacher training. A baby a year, well, nobody in her backwoods family had taught her how to manage that. Meg was her mother's fifth live birth when the stock market crashed in 1929. Meg had been one baby too many for her overwhelmed mother, that much Meg knew. But she never knew exactly what had happened.

The driving sounds of the waterfall up ahead reached her, so she slowed her walk in order to be silent. Only Arthur would use the swimming hole on Baptism Sunday. Everyone else would have headed off to Valois Castle or Watkins, depending on who they wanted to see. She tiptoed from mounds of soft moss onto bent ferns. She lifted the hem of her shirtwaist to protect it from prickers on branches. When the top of the waterfall came into view, she heard a thunk, then a splash. She crouched low, sneaking behind the thicker growth. The swimming hole shone like a polished stone. Suddenly Arthur's head emerged and he flipped over onto his back, naked, and floated. Meg held her breath. If she moved at all, he might hear.

She memorized what she saw. How odd that she wasn't embarrassed or uncomfortable, but still she wouldn't want him to know she was there. She would wait till he made enough noise to cover hers; then she would leave. And then he would never know.

But when Arthur finally did move, she couldn't leave. He had flipped onto his front, baring his back to the sky, revealing welts the size of fists or rocks near his kidneys.

Meg stared. Even at a distance, the purple wounds contrasted his smooth skin. She knew who had done it. Cowards. They knew Arthur wouldn't tell. And his overalls would hide the evidence. Her eyes stung.

Did Hank know? Was it his idea?

Arthur frog-kicked to the rim of the swimming hole and slid onto a slate ledge, using his arms to keep his back stiff, flinching when he pulled too hard. Then he lay there on his belly so the sun could dry him.

She knew she should leave, but the moss had allowed her feet to sink. Her arms cradled her shoes while a breeze rustled leaves above her and she watched Arthur rest.

Finally, she turned to go. Gram would wonder why she'd stayed away so long. She hadn't meant to disobey. She'd just forgotten.

The farther she walked, the less carefully she picked her steps. She kept worrying about direct sunlight on Arthur's wounds. If they dried out and cracked, they might get infected. A pricker caught the arch of her foot, so she found a stump to sit on and removed it. With the flat of her hand, she wiped a dot of blood, which she licked. She applied pressure with her thumb till a clot started, then laid a green leaf over the spot and tucked her foot into her shoe.

When she looked up, Arthur stood close by, watching her, buttoning his shirt over his overalls. She blushed. Neither of them spoke.

They wandered among the trees toward home. White butterflies danced above the wild strawberries where the bees had been and the scent of skunk still lingered.

"You shouldn't come out here alone," Arthur said. "You can't be sure what you might see."

"Maybe you ought to wear a bathing suit." She glanced at him, but he watched the path ahead. He didn't care that she'd seen him without his clothes on, she knew that.

"Where'd you get the welts?"

"Fell. Wrestling Ol' Pete."

He gently took her hand. Crickets chirruped. Sunlight brightened the woods' canopy as they neared the Lees' property line. He paused.

"I'll wait a while," he said, letting go of her hand. "You leave first."

She looked up. Why after so many years of thinking of him as a brother, as a pesky brother even, why suddenly did she feel so differently standing near him? She knew Gram was waiting. But she suddenly loathed the Wickhams and she couldn't tell anyone why.

She touched a top button on his shirt. His chest rose and fell with soft breaths. She tucked a strand of wet hair behind his ear. Their foreheads pressed together, his hair falling forward around their faces.

Their noses touched. Then their lips. She dangled her arms at her sides so she wouldn't bump his sores.

Chapter 4

Meg slipped inside the door to the cool saloon. Strands of light from an open window lit dust particles in mid-air. She ignored two figures at the bar and padded softly along the wood floor toward the back stairs, holding her breath to dodge the scent of lye and liquor. Her slip-on shoes hid her hands like mittens.

"Hank Wickham's up there," Charley announced from behind the bar. "Got here nigh on twenty minutes ago."

She stopped at the foot of the stairs. Lye tingled the lining of her nose now. Her eyes had begun to adjust to the dark, and she could see the other figure at the bar was Charley's sister, Sally, slumped forward on a stool. Her gray hair clung to her scalp. A towel hugged the shoulders of her wet cotton dress.

"Thanks." Meg stepped into her shoes. She brushed imaginary wrinkles out of her skirt, then saw a tiny spot of blood, smudged off Arthur's shirt onto her waistband.

"Best go rescue him," Charley said. "Your Gramps'll scare him off with all them pointers on that tractor o' his."

"Yes." Meg faked a giggle. The sounds of small talk trickled down from the closed door at the top of the stairs. She pictured Hank seated, maybe in Gram's rocker by the window, one lanky leg crossed over the other. He would smile every time Gram interrupted Gramps to offer glass after glass of lemonade. Grownups liked Hank. Meg wished she had stayed longer in the woods as she climbed the stairs to the flat.

"Well, here she is!" Gram rose from her rocker, beaming as she did on Christmas mornings. Samantha slid from her arms to the chair, then the floor. "Lookey who stopped by!"

Hank bounded up off the couch and dwarfed the room in his pressed uniform. He bowed his head and waited while Gramps wriggled from side to side to leverage himself against the coffee table and stand, slightly bent at the waist.

"Hello, Meg," Hank said.

"Hi ya."

"Your grandmother's asked me to drive you over the other side of the lake. Nice day for a drive. We can take the Ford." He stood proud, his hat in one hand, his smile plump but masculine against his freshly shaved face. Meg felt numb.

"Your Aunt Lizzie's got them watermelon rinds ready," Gram explained. "Gramps saw Cousin Nora over to the dunking—I mean, the baptism."

Gramps winked at Meg, which Hank noted with a grin.

"Lizzie's got 'em ready for your mother," Gram said. "Bet they're good."

"I've heard talk of those pickled watermelon rinds." Hank flashed his nicely aligned teeth at Meg. "Sure would like to taste one myself."

"Yes."

Special food requests from her mother hadn't stumped Meg like this in a long time. Now that she rarely spoke to her sisters, and with her brother in Europe, she hardly ever thought about daily life at her parents' house.

"Fantastic," Hank said. "Ford's parked just down the hill. All right if we walk to it?" He waited for Meg to answer. "Or I can go get it, if you like."

"Nice day for a walk," Gramps said.

"Real nice," said Gram.

Meg kept picturing Arthur in the forest just minutes ago. She noticed dust particles in the air of Gram's bright flat, especially around Hank's head, where light from the window gathered them into a ring.

Maybe he really didn't know what his brother had done to Arthur. Maybe Hank had been too busy seeing to his cousin, getting himself to church with his parents one last time before shipping out, then rushing over to see her. He'd be leaving in a day or two for the war. If only Aunt Lizzie's watermelon rinds weren't ready, she could just sit and drink lemonade with him here on Gramps' couch.

Gram waddled toward the door and pulled it open. Sam stood beside her, purring.

"I can come back later," Hank said softly. "Kinda rude to show up uninvited. Especially after I missed you last night. I'm sorry."

At school he'd had a way of corralling every teacher's sympathy. Now Gram swayed at the door, and Gramps harrumphed.

"Thanks," Meg said. "I'd be grateful for a ride to Aunt Lizzie's." She willed as hard as she could for Arthur to be working in the barn now so he wouldn't see her.

Hank glanced over her mussed hair, her dress, her

scuffed shoes. She folded her hands at her waist to cover the blood spot on her skirt.

"Great," he said. "Let's go."

Outside, only a few parishioners lingered in front of the church. Otherwise, the highway and neighborhood seemed empty. But her daddy was sure to be watching, and maybe some other sets of eyes. She felt like the emperor in invisible clothes.

"It's down the road here a piece."

Hank angled onto a dirt path that merged with the road toward the lake. He swung himself in a half circle to let her catch up. His stride drove their pace, but then he checked himself, as if herding her, keeping her close while nudging her forward.

Cornflower blue dusted the edge of cornfields down the hill. The lake twinkled into view. A steady insect drone overpowered the sounds of frogs and gulls. The fields brought back Arthur's earthen smell, his wet hair. She shook her head to set the memory free, but it clung to her like incense.

"Here's Woodie," Hank said. He scooted ahead to open the passenger door of his father's Ford. When Meg crouched to climb inside, he asked, "You okay?" and she bumped her head at the top of the door opening.

"Here." He slid his hand under her arm and with long fingers guided her down onto the warm leather seat. The car smelled of tobacco and spicy cologne. He lowered himself to his haunches outside her door and looked up into her face, his elbows on his knees. A soft breeze off the fields ruffled his hair. "You all right?"

His intense stare made her skin tingle. She tapped her temple. "Headache."

"Too much dancing last night?" He winked.

His smile seemed genuine enough, but something made her wonder. She'd rarely faced anyone this clever before, except for Gram, who was sharper than everyone.

"I got home late," he said. He placed his hand on the dash in front of her to balance himself and frowned. His breath had an acid smell. "Heard at breakfast how you danced. I'm glad for it. Sorry I wasn't there."

The cornflowers in the field behind him rippled, and she wondered if he knew what Al had done to Arthur. Then she sank deeper into the leather seat, hoping the dashboard might camouflage her when they drove up the road through Valois.

"You should work in a war office," she murmured. He laughed. "You're smart. They could use that."

He swung himself upright. "Think it's gonna be like a Hollywood movie, do you?" He clicked her door shut, chuckling, and stepped around the front of the Ford.

Meg watched his uniform contour to his body as he sauntered toward the driver's seat. It was hard to picture him aiming a gun at Germans, hunkered in a trench with damp socks, following orders he disagreed with. Had he ever gone hungry for more than a day? His family had prospered, even during the Crash. She was sure he'd always slept in a cozy bed.

"Why didn't we do this sooner?" His voice was low as he settled into the car and turned the key in the ignition. He let the engine idle and stretched his arm across the back of the seat. "Why did I wait to notice you now, just when I'm leaving? How smart was that?"

He leaned toward her, but she rubbed her temple. He waited. She stared at the glove compartment, conscious of a remnant scent of algae lingering on her hair, from the swimming hole, from Arthur's hair. She wished Hank would stop looking at her.

Finally he coughed, straightened up, and reached for a Camel pack on the dash. He tapped out a cigarette without offering her one and fumbled with the car's metal lighter, exhaling out the side of his mouth through the driver's window. He shifted the car into gear and sighed.

"Need an aspirin?"

She shook her head no.

He pulled onto the road, stirring up a cloud of dust behind them.

****

The road to Aunt Lizzie's flanked the east side of the lake. Cornstalks stood at attention like an army of scarecrows. An August breeze marshaled clouds to the west, as if a battle raged just below the horizon.

Hank and Meg saw few other cars on their trek, just a couple when they sped through Watkins. But even in town, Sunday dinners and lazy after-dessert naps kept most people indoors. On the road up to the Graebners' farm, the Wickham Ford strewed dust like dun-colored paint.

Meg knocked twice on the wood frame of the screen door to Aunt Lizzie's farmhouse. Cows slumbered in the nearby pasture, dissolved into the landscape like heaps of mud.

"H'lo?"

A door squeaked open from the back of the house. Lizzie Graebner emerged, her girth a younger version of Gram's. Her waist-length braid was knotted at the nape of her neck. Meg knew this braid would come undone that night and be worked through with a fine-toothed comb.

"Got my message, did'ja?" Lizzie splayed her arms. She hugged Meg and kissed her on the lips. "And who have we here?"

Meg presented Hank as she would a quilt she'd made, stepping back and spreading her arms. Lizzie eyed him head to toe.

"Haven't seen you since you was wee. Wouldn't 'a' know'd you." She held out her hand. He took hold to shake it, but she just held on. "Knew your dad in school years ago. Right smart fella."

"Yes, ma'am. Heard about your pickled watermelon rinds. Hoping to taste one."

"Well, come on!" She pulled him by the hand toward the shed. "You're in for a treat, if I do say it."

Meg strayed to the far side of the house, where she could see her Uncle Jim riding his tractor in the distance. She waved her arms till he waved back. Thunder rumbled from the west, where a shelf of clouds was mounting. A vague breeze shuffled the air. She wandered slowly back to the shed.

"Lordy, these are good." Hank held out an open jar to Meg.

Lizzie's dim workshop smelled of sweet apples and hay. Crates and cardboard boxes of glass jars littered work tables and most of the floor. Tools and empty jars crowded plywood shelves.

"Got the clove balanced to the vinegar just right this year," Lizzie said, her hands folded across her abdomen, a twin gesture to Gram's. "And the sugar. Boiled it proper. Not too sour."

Meg bit into the cool, slimy pickle. Spices mixed

with cider meant fall was coming, the start of another school year. The return of sweaters and early sundowns. Another set of boys would be sent off to war.

"Take this'un to your mother," Lizzie said, pointing to a loaded cardboard box.

"I'll get it," Hank said.

"Well, hold on." Lizzie touched his arm. "Here's one for you." She pointed to a larger, heavier crate. "You two split this big'un. Half to Gram and half to Miz Wickham." She patted his shoulder. "Give your folks my regards. And be careful. Awful smart, them Germans. Watch your back over there. Come home safe."

"Yes, ma'am. I will." Hank winked and held up a jar. "Think I'll sneak some of these on the ship."

Lizzie's eyes teared up. Meg had seen this happen to Gram lots of times. She always assumed it was because of the two babies Gram had lost to typhoid back when Daddy and Lizzie were children. But Meg wondered why Lizzie sometimes teared up too.

Meg suspected more women had miscarriages than let on. She knew her mother'd had several because Ron had told her. "I remember Daddy carrying the pot of blood," Ron had said. "Two times, at least." Maybe Lizzie'd had some secret losses too.

Meg hugged her aunt. "I waved to Uncle Jim."

"Rain's a comin', or he'd come in."

"I know." Meg puckered her lips and kissed Lizzie on the lips. "Alfalfa's rich this year, Mr. Lee says."

"Sure is." Lizzie followed Meg and Hank to the Ford, where they lowered their boxes into the trunk. Lizzie ran her finger along the wood siding. "H'ain't seen one of these up close before." She clasped her hands behind her back and poked her head inside the passenger's window. "Fancy."

"Like a ride?" Hank asked.

Lizzie shook her finger no and backed away toward the house.

"You two get going before the rain come." She eyed the horizon. "Sometime by sundown, I expect."

"You'll take a 'rain check'?" Hank called.

Lizzie giggled and waved them away.

The Ford lumbered over bumps in the dirt road while seagulls honked weather forecasts. A cow and her calf sheltered themselves under a tree.

"You could drop off a jar to your cousin," Meg offered. "Might cheer him up."

"That's a swell idea." Hank glanced to the west. "Think the weather'll hold off a couple more hours?"

"Sure."

They drove through Watkins again, passing the sign for Elmira.

"Mrs. B took us to Elmira on a field trip last spring," Meg said.

"She did, did she?"

"Yep."

Meg and Greta had strolled in hushed reverence around Mark Twain's summer home, Quarry Farm, where he penned *Huckleberry Finn* and *The Prince and the Pauper*. And for Meg and Greta, silence was not natural. But they felt they walked on hallowed ground.

"Ever hear of John Jones?" Meg asked.

Hank shook his head.

"Mrs. B showed us the cemetery he used to work at. He helped people catch the Underground Railroad at Elmira to Niagara Falls, and then up to Canada."

"Uh-huh." Hank steered with his elbow and lit a Camel.

"He'd been a slave himself. Bought a farm. Did real well. None of the folks he helped ever got caught."

"Think that was his real name?" He exhaled out the driver's window.

Meg hadn't considered otherwise. "I don't know. John Jones."

Hank shrugged. "Sounds made up."

Meg thought it over. She wanted to say probably lots of folks changed their names when they came North to escape slavery, but she didn't. "You should work in one of those interrogation rooms."

He laughed. "Think I could fish the truth out of Krauts, do you? Wish I was as smart as you think I am." He took another drag on his cigarette, steering the car up the stretch of highway along the east side of the lake.

"I leave first thing tomorrow morning," he told her. "Then we ship outta Camp Shanks on the nineteenth."

"Where to," she asked.

"Germany, I think. Following your brother Ron's footsteps."

In a normal year, her brother would be training for his annual deer hunting expedition. Come November, he'd join Arthur, with his truck stocked with water, rifles, and parched corn, the perfect snack for staving off hunger in the Allegheny woods.

In a normal year they'd return filthy, euphoric, their fingernails caked with dry blood, their limit of one deer each piled lifeless in the bed of the truck. Then there would be Gram's stew in winter. Or hunks of Viv's roast, rushed steaming across the street by Ron, who'd stay to eat, then scoot back home for double dippings. Meg always felt conflicted eating venison. But Arthur would have thanked the deers' spirits after each kill. Eating the meat was good luck, he said.

She stared out her window at the August trees, the edges of their leaves crisping, preparing to fall. She tried not to think of her brother shooting boys his own age, how it would haunt him at night. Different than hunting bucks.

"It'll go quick now," Hank said. "With Paris liberated, should be a matter of weeks. Soon's I get over there, they'll be sending me back home."

The Ford was nearing the turn-off for Ithaca. Afternoon light was fading to a dull gray and soon a chill would set in. Meg rolled her window up halfway. Arthur's grandmother's words came back to her, and she smiled, then sighed.

"What?" Hank said.

"Oh, nothing."

"What?" Hank pressed.

"Something somebody said about Hitler."

"What?"

"The Iroquois," she hesitated. "They have their own name for him."

"Well?"

"He who smells his moustache."

He smiled briefly. "I may borrow that." Then he tossed the remains of his cigarette out the window and steered the Ford onto the dirt road to Ithaca, a single lane with deep ruts. "Isn't Arthur nineteen? Why doesn't he enlist?"

"Mr. Lee needs him on the farm. He's only eighteen." She wondered again what Hank knew about

Al and Arthur.

Hank ran his fingers through his hair.

"Somebody's got to grow food for the troops," she said. "That's what Mr. Lee says." She'd heard Gramps say it, too. Much as he hated Hitler, Gramps hated seeing boys go to war more. Saying good-bye to her brother, Gramps wiped his face again and again on his flannel sleeve. She'd never seen him like that before.

Of all the local boys, Arthur would make the best soldier. He was sturdier, more sensible under pressure, more likely to come back alive. But she was glad he was safe at the farm.

They drove past the water tower at Trumansburg, and before long Cayuga Lake appeared to the east. The sun lit up Ithaca, on the far shore. Cornell stood like a fortress on the hillside, separate from the downtown saloons, shops, and vaudeville house.

"My cousin's at our grandparents', up State Street. After I drop this, we could drive through campus, if you like."

"Swell."

Meg had never seen Cornell up close before. She studied the colorful Victorian homes along State Street as they climbed the steep hill.

"Folks sure live on top of each other."

Hank chuckled. "Every place seems like that after Valois."

Hank's grandparents lived in a three-story manor house with a wide veranda and a sloping front lawn. Meg waited in the car while Hank ran a jar up to a carved antique door. A slender matron greeted him with a stiff kiss, her gray hair arranged in a French twist. Hank backed away quickly, waving. Halfway down the lawn, he cupped his hand to his mouth and shouted toward an open window on the third floor.

"Heal fast, you fool!"

"Kill me a Kraut, brother!" Hank's cousin called from inside the open window.

Hank shook his head when he started the engine. "I signed up with him in Pennsylvania so we could be together over there. All that training for nothing. Damn shame."

Chapter 5

They motored down State, then onto College Avenue. Homes were suddenly unkempt, with paint peeling off rotting wood. Yards of weeds and dirt patches sported rose bushes thick with thorns. Tree roots sprouted cracks in the sidewalks.

"Student housing," Hank said. He pointed to a ramshackle Victorian with Greek lettering above the door. "My dad's fraternity."

"He went here?"

"I will too, when I get back. Uncle Sam's footing the bill. Dad and his buddies, they pushed hard for that. Those Legionaires, signing petitions and what not. I'm grateful to them."

Meg watched Hank's distant stare as the car edged along the road. "That'll be a big help to you boys when you come home," she offered.

"Yep," he said, shifting in his seat and forcing a smile. "I had a state scholarship already, but I guess I won't need that now."

Small shops and eateries appeared. Then Cornell's campus came into view. At the end of the tree-lined street, a soaring clock tower stood forth on the hill above the lake.

"Let's park. I'll take you in the libe. Uris Tower."

A cement pathway led them past seasoned brick buildings, the kind she imagined at Oxford or

Cambridge. Or as Mr. Rochester's mansion in *Jane Eyre*. Lush poplars and oaks filtered the sunshine. A statue of a man with Lincolnesque whiskers, wearing a knee-length frock coat, stared down on them.

"That's Ezra." Hank slowed his lope. "'I will found a university where any person can find instruction in any study.' Something like that. He was related to Ben Franklin. Remotely, anyway. Of course, I guess a lot of people were, huh?" He poked her with his elbow and chuckled. She pretended to miss his point and continued to gaze at the statue.

"Started off poor, though, ol' Ezra." He shrugged. "Sold plows for a living." He took hold of her elbow. "Better keep moving. We'll be driving back into weather."

"How'd he end up with all this?"

"Western Union. Got lucky when the telegraph was new. Saw an opportunity and seized it. Smart man."

He guided her up stone steps to the library. Inside, he steered her away from the brightly lit main room and up a dim flight of stairs. He pulled open a door with a stained-glass window. Inside, a grand picture window lined with plush armchairs opened onto a full vista of Cayuga Lake. Metal staircases twisted in spirals to tiered stacks lined with books. Shelves barricaded private desks stationed at windows. The dense carpet absorbed sound. Students lounged, engrossed in their books. Some slept.

"C'mon," Hank whispered and turned back toward the door. She hesitated.

Why did these posh surroundings feel familiar? She lifted a stray volume from the corner of a stack and turned its careworn pages. Maybe when she graduated high school she could apply for a job re-shelving books. Eventually she could become a librarian and sneak up to this room on her breaks. She might ask to live at Hank's grandparents' in exchange for house cleaning and laundry chores. She'd take the bus or walk to work. It wasn't far. She'd wait tables in Collegetown for extra money.

"Let's go," Hank whispered.

She tried to memorize the dusty smell of the stacks, the view of the lake, a stuffed chair so soft it could engulf a body and never let go.

They left the upper room, then exited through the vestibule to the outdoors again. He circled to the downhill foot of the clock tower and paused outside a heavy oak portal.

"Here. Ready? It's one heck of a climb!"

Inside he raced up a narrow spiral staircase. She followed at her own pace. Once she stopped to allow two students to pass on their way down. The girl's spiked heels caught in the holes of the metal steps. The boy wore glasses with lenses thick as Coke bottles.

"Come on!" Hank called. "We've got a storm to beat!"

"Coming!"

At the top, Hank waited at the west side of a walkway which circled a massive bell. Meg leaned her head out a glassless opening for fresh air, but the sight of the ground below gave her jitters, then nausea. The view spun.

"Okay?" He came to her and took hold of her shoulders. "Got the willies?" He laughed into her eyes till she regained focus. "I've got you." He clutched her hand firmly. His Camel breath was like a grownup's.

"Not much for heights, are you?" He led her slowly to the west side of the walkway. "Look out far. That'll help."

She let go his hand and gripped the railings. He stood back.

The charcoal weather in the west contrasted Ithaca's glow. Silence hung inside the musty tower. The shuffle of a shoe seemed out of place. Seagulls over the Arts Quad sounded far away.

Hank moved beside her and slowly placed a hand on her waist. He leaned his chin in her hair where the trace of algae lingered.

"We'd better go," she said.

She slipped away.

He strode past her, avoiding her eyes, but his neck and cheeks were flushed. His hands were thrust deep into his pockets.

"Going down's easy," he said.

Why did his touch feel cool and strange? And why had Hank suddenly taken an interest in her anyway? Until today they had rarely spoken. He and Jessie Mae Burke had gone together all through high school. Blonde Jessie Mae, well-off like Hank, and a good student, too. Everyone assumed they'd get married one day.

How had Meg gone from being a girl who'd never had a boyfriend to suddenly having two boys like her at the same time?

They drove out of town in silence. Navy stripes of cloud splintered orange rays above the fields. Meg rolled her window up except for a slim crack.

"Cornell's wonderful," she said.

"You should apply."

She fingered the leather car seat and wondered what life felt like for people who didn't worry about money all the time.

"Go after the state scholarship," he said casually. "I'm not using it."

"What is it?"

"The New York State scholarship. Then when I get back you can invite me to your sorority house." He sighed, then added, "Seriously, I was gonna ask if I could write you while I'm away."

She waited for him to say more, but he didn't. He glanced at her and appeared ready to reach for a cigarette, but his hands remained on the wheel. A flock of sparrows gushed up from a nearby field. The western clouds were spreading into a ceiling of smoky gray.

"Sure," she heard herself say. She wasn't certain, though, and smoothed her hair. What harm could it do? She just didn't know.

The Ford slowed when the sign for Trumansburg appeared. Painted shutters protected closed windows. Wind spurts swirled batches of leaves along the deserted sidewalk. At the turn-off to the water tower, raindrops the size of gumdrops pebbled the windshield. Meg cranked the window closed.

An explosive crack boomed overhead, followed soon by a gold streak against the blackened horizon. Hank veered onto the narrow road through Interlaken. Rain tapped the Ford's roof like quick drumbeats. Hank frowned, wrestling the steering wheel to keep the Ford from sliding into deep wet ruts.

"Hino's out," she said.

"Huh?"

"Hino'Hoha. Thunder's son."

"Hino-who?" Hank stared forward, perspiration gathering above his lip.

The sound of the lightning came quicker after each flash. Meg searched for a patch of blue up ahead, but rain grayed out any view beyond a few yards in front of the Ford.

"An old woman had seven daughters," Meg began, leaning closer for him to hear, to help him stay focused while he kept the car out of the ditch. "The seventh daughter died but left a baby boy by her grave."

"Where'd you hear this?"

"Arthur. He used to tell Greta and me his grandma's stories when we were little."

He sighed again. Irritated or bored, she supposed. But Meg followed her urge to tell him the myth.

"The grandmother was poor, so poor you couldn't tell what kind of animal her blanket had once been."

"A weasel?"

"Too small," she said. His face relaxed a little. "Probably a buffalo or a bear. Anyway, it turns out the boy's father was Hino, which means thunder. And the story tells how Thunder Boy had to win games at dice to survive."

"Sounds like the great bowling alley in the sky."

The fields around them had vanished. The car drove blind in a capsule surrounded by fog. Meg prayed they wouldn't meet a car coming from the opposite direction.

"Every time Hino'Hoha won at dice," she said, "he cut off the loser's head."

"Arthur told you that?"

"The best part is when Hino'Hoha's uncle is trapped under a tree, with roots growing across his neck and feet. Hino'Hoha saved him."

By the time the road finally curved and spilled onto the paved state highway, the rainfall had slackened. After a hundred yards, the Ford pulled alongside Meg's parents' house. Lightning zigzagged across the lake, followed by a deafening crash.

"Let me bring the pickle jars in the morning before I leave," Hank said. Her wrist pressed down on her door handle. She shook her head.

"I'll get them fast," she said. "Give the big one to your folks. We don't need any."

He took hold of her arm. "Wait a minute. Don't run off. Please."

Maybe it was the closed windows that made her head hurt. The rain pounded the roof.

"Okay if I write?" He reached for her far hand, the one resting on the door handle. She made herself let him take it. "You'll write back?"

"Sure."

He licked his lips and gently tugged her closer to him. But she pulled away.

"Be careful over there," she said in earnest.

Then she slid out of the car into pouring rain.

He met her at the trunk and hoisted the box of jars, ready to carry it himself to the door. But Meg wrested it from him like a cherished toy. There was a loud thunder crack and she scurried up the steps into her parents' house.

She would remember him slack-jawed, his drenched wool coat molded to him like old skin.

****

Daddy's smoke had collected. The windows were shut tight against the storm. Table lamps flickered near his stuffed chair and at Mother's piano, a baby grand cluttered with sheet music and newspapers.

"Hi ya, Daddy." Meg wiped her feet on the doormat, hugging the soaked cardboard box.

He coughed and released a cat from his lap to the floor. "Catch your death, if you're not careful. June's spendin' the night over to the depot, roads're so bad." His cigarette hung low between his fingers, to the side of his chair. He puckered his lips.

She walked to his chair and struggled around the box to kiss his leathery mouth. When she straightened up, he smiled broadly, his thick lips spread over square, yellowed teeth.

"Hank Wickham, Meg. Mercy." He patted the box. "Take that in to Viv."

Meg ventured into the kitchen, where boiled beef, onions, and tomatoes stewed, masking the wallpaper's mold, the wooden floor's layers of too many stray paws, too many boot soles packed with axle grease, mud, and manure. Only one homemade electric lamp lit the room.

"Smell's good, Viv." She set the box on the chopping block in the center of the room.

"Better get home to Gram's for a hot bath," Viv said, ever apt to ignore a compliment, "before you catch your death and miss the start of school."

"Think I could take a pickle up to Mom?"

Viv shook her head.

"Had a bad day today. She's asleep. Doctor brought over some pills. Maybe it's Ron being in France, I don't know. Here we go again."

Meg's heart sank. Her mother had seemed much better lately. Viv nodded toward a tin by the back door.

Several black umbrellas with broken spokes stood in it, ready for trips to the outhouse.

"Grab one of those," she said. "And get on home to Gram's. June's camping out at the depot. I'm tryin' to keep the house quiet so Mom can stay home. Once they check her in at the ward, takes forever to get her back out."

Chapter 6

Two weeks drifted by. Meg worked most days at Chef's. Few customers came in, so she scrubbed floors and countertops to keep busy. In the evenings she strolled with Greta to the lakefront and sometimes took a dip. One night, she couldn't wait any longer and asked, "Where's Arthur?"

"Penn Yan," Greta said. "Helping his uncle bring in the alfalfa. Then he has to go to Buffalo to see his mother."

"But he'll miss the first day of school! This is the problem, just like I've told him over and over. This is why he falls behind."

"He quit school," Greta said, then shifted the conversation to college applications and other such matters.

****

Meg fretted in bed that night. Did Arthur quit school because of Al and his bullies? Then it was her fault. Or was he planning to enlist? She dreaded him going to war more than anyone. She kept imagining herself at his funeral, his grandmother wearing a black shawl, hovering over an oblong hole in the ground at the Seneca Union Cemetery.

And then Great Aunt May's face would flash in her mind, like a weird waking dream. Silent, chalk white in that oak coffin lined with satin. Gram holding her down close enough to smell formaldehyde, which at three years old she knew wasn't the smell of her dear Auntie.

Why was Auntie quiet and stiff? They'd been playing puzzles just a day or so ago. And why couldn't she live with Uncle Roy anymore? Gram was nice, but Gramps never played. Uncle Roy read nursery rhymes at bedtime. Why did everyone whisper?

****

A cobalt sky topped the day before the start of senior year. Meg dressed quickly for work that morning to make time for coffee at Greta's before catching the bus to Watkins. Black-Eyed Susans waved. The grass was still damp from rain the night before.

"Morning, Miz Lee," Meg said, letting herself in through the back screen door.

"Morning, Meg." Mrs. Lee called in the direction of the front bedroom, "Gret?" She set her newspaper aside and closed her silk wrapper. "Excuse our screaming."

"Ye-es?" came a yell.

"Meg's here!" Mrs. Lee chuckled. "Coffee?"

"Yes, thanks. I'll get it."

"Heard from your brother?"

"Telegram from France."

Mrs. Lee beamed. "Wonderful."

"Yes."

Paris liberated. Her brother Ron alive, serving his country proud.

A china bowl of peaches sat beside a sliced loaf of black bread. Meg's favorite embroidered napkins flanked hand-painted plates and silver knives, next to a plate of soft butter.

Greta appeared at the kitchen entrance. "Hand me a

cup of Mother's brew. Gosh, it's so early." She looped a white ribbon around her ponytail.

"Good practice for tomorrow," Mrs. Lee said.

"Oh, why must they start school so early? It's un-American!"

"One lump or two?" Meg asked.

"Four."

Mrs. Lee peeled a peach. A Gershwin tune played on the radio.

"May I have that?" Greta held her hand out for the coil of peach fuzz. "Give Meg the rest."

"So soft," Meg said. "Not tart at all."

"They've been sitting in a basket," Mrs. Lee said. "Must be that's the secret. Arthur picked them before he left."

Meg chewed the juicy peach, wishing she'd talked to Arthur before he left. She'd never explained about Hank. Arthur must've seen the Ford parked in front of her parents' house in the rain.

"Mother said she'll take us to a show tonight," Greta said.

"To launch your senior year," said Mrs. Lee. "For good luck."

"Like to?" Greta asked. "*The White Cliffs of Dover*? Remember Ms. B teaching us Alice Duer Miller?"

"Oh, the suffragette," Meg said. "Yes."

"It's based on her poem. And we love Irene Dunne. It'll be swell!"

****

While Allied forces paraded the streets of Paris on the giant screen, Meg scanned the audience, lit by spill from the film at the Grand State Theatre. She noticed

Jessie Mae Burke sitting with her friend Annette in a nearby row. Jessie Mae's white-blonde hair, usually so carefully brushed and coiffed, seemed messy, slightly neglected. When the newsreel ended, Jessie Mae stood, her head bent low, and exited up the main aisle. But she moved slowly, stiffly, not in her usual vivacious way. Annette followed after her. Meg and Greta glanced at each other, then at Mrs. Lee, who gazed straight ahead at the movie screen.

Was Jessie Mae worried about Hank at war? Why had Hank broken up with her anyway, or was it her idea? None of it seemed right. Meg felt a pang she didn't think she deserved. She'd never flirted with Hank, at least not on purpose, although she'd noticed him, like all the girls. And she'd giggled at his jokes, though she never thought they were good. Then a month ago, when he invited her out over the cash register, she felt like Lana Turner, discovered. It hadn't occurred to her then to wonder about Jessie Mae. Or to wonder why he'd suddenly chosen her, Meg Michaels, a fifteen-year-old bookworm.

Irene Dunne stood beside her son's hospital bed, at a window, brave in her nurse's uniform, watching the Americans' victory parade. Then Peter Lawford closed his eyes and died. Mrs. Lee passed tissues to Greta and Meg.

"Oh, why did she let him go to war?" Greta wailed in the car on the way home. "Why did she listen to Roddy McDowall and not leave England? That was too sad, watching Peter Lawford die. He should have been in more of the movie!"

"I had trouble, too," Meg leaned forward from the back seat. "Believing she'd let her son fight after she lost her husband in the Great War? And it wasn't her country, even."

"It was her adopted country, though," Mrs. Lee said. "Someone has to fight the wars, girls."

Meg pushed away thoughts of losing her brother or any of the local boys. Sure, she was patriotic, but she recognized something of her mother in herself. A tendency to panic. She tried to think of something else.

"But now she's all alone," Greta kept wailing. "It's too sad. She was so beautiful and in love. And her husband was nice and he could dance. And now she's all alone with the nuns."

Mrs. Lee sighed. The car slowed as it passed through Trumansburg. The sky above them was dense with stars.

Meg cast wishes for her brother Ron and for Hank: please send them home safely. Then she wished on the brightest star at the horizon for Arthur to stay home. The chant of crickets through the car's open window echoed: Stay home, Arthur; Arthur, stay home.

She made a wish for her mother, too. One she didn't think could ever come true.

****

When they reached Valois, she thanked Mrs. Lee and Greta, and slipped inside the saloon. Charley's Labrador thumped her tail on the floor.

"It's just me, Brandy."

Now that her puppies were due, Brandy slept behind the bar on a towel. She'd always lived outside before, but Charley wanted her close to his back room, in case she needed him in the night.

Meg crept upstairs. The apartment was dark except for the light Gram had left on in her room. Samantha's steady breathing serenaded her from the couch. She wandered into the dark kitchen for a glass of milk, leaning on her elbows by the sink, peering out the window. The moon's haze over the Lee house resembled a scene from Alfred Hitchcock's *Shadow of a Doubt*.

"They shoot the movie in daylight," her brother Ron had explained once. "Then they overexpose the film and it looks like night. 'Day for night' they call it."

She spotted Arthur's truck parked in the Lee's driveway, almost hidden by Mrs. Lee's car and a strange jalopy behind it.

Was he back? She found herself stealing out of the apartment, back down the stairs, causing Brandy's tail to thump again.

She tried to reason with herself. What if Mrs. Lee sat in her kitchen in the dark, too, stirred by the movie, staring out the window? What if she saw Meg sneak to the barn? And maybe Arthur wasn't sleeping in the barn anyway. But he would be. When his grandmother had company, he gave up his room. And the car in the driveway couldn't belong to a guest of the Lee's. Too shabby.

It was only eleven. She could be home by midnight and still sharp enough for school in the morning. If someone caught her, she'd say she left her wallet in Mrs. Lee's car. By way of the barn? Well, she'd figure that part out if she had to.

She ran as if speed would make her invisible. No lights glowed from the Lee's house or Arthur's grandmother's. She slowed her pace when she neared the barn. The door opened easily. Sweet hay rustled under the quiet grumble of cows and Ol' Pete. Across from the middle stall, moonlight lit the ladder to the hayloft.

"Arthur!" Meg's whisper carried easily through the barn. She stepped farther inside. "Arthur!"

He appeared at the top of the ladder, shirtless, kneeling in his blue jeans, pulling straw from his ponytail. His face was in shadow.

She stifled a grin, feeling the moonlight on her face, and clasped her hands behind her back.

"Hello," she said.

He rubbed his eyes. "Why ain't you in bed?"

"Can't sleep. Why are you sleeping out here?"

He shifted himself to a sitting position and dangled his legs at the side of the ladder. His face caught the moonlight. "My mom and her husband are here. Just stayin' the night."

"'You mean your stepdad?"

"Well, I don't think of him as such."

"Don't like him?"

"Not much." He rubbed under his arm and yawned.

She calculated the time he'd been away. Was it three full weeks? He already looked more man than boy. The single fold across his stomach, made from sitting, grabbed her attention.

"Are you coming down, or should I come up?"

"You shouldn't be here," he said.

For the first time it occurred to her that he might not want to see her. Would he give her a chance to explain about Hank? She'd always assumed she was pretty enough, but what if she was wrong about that? What if he thought of her as a kid sister?

"C'mon up," he said.

He moved back into the hayloft while she climbed

the wooden rungs. He was kneeling on a blanket in the loose straw, settled back on his haunches, his hands folded on his lap. She knelt down in front of him on the blanket.

"I've been thinking, Meg."

She pictured him pitching alfalfa, wishing her out of his life. Or driving the long miles back from Buffalo, planning how he'd tell her she wasn't worth the trouble she'd caused.

"Maybe we should just be friends," he said.

Her belly ached. "If you don't like me, Arthur, just say so."

"It's not that."

"You can say it. I can take it."

He smiled and shook his head. "It's Al. I swear he ain't normal."

"We should tell somebody. The police." She knew he wouldn't. But how could he just let it be? "You didn't fight back, did you."

"I break someone's neck, I go to jail. It ain't worth it." He stared at his knees, his hands on his thighs, then glanced back at her with a look that reminded her of Gramps, and even Samantha. "It ain't right, you and me, anyway."

"Why?"

"You know why."

"Everybody's pressing me. And I just don't want that, that's all."

"Pressing you?"

She wanted to mention Hank's name, but she couldn't. "You shouldn't quit school, you know."

"I'm too old now. Mr. Lee needs my help."

"School won't be the same if you're not there."

62

His head sank. Then he told her again, gently, "We should just stay friends, Meg. The most I'll ever be is a farmer, if I'm lucky. I ain't for you."

He'd already slipped away and made his mind up without her during the past weeks. Could she coax him back?

"My mother's not so good again," she said.

"Oh." He sighed a long breath. "Sorry."

Why was she using her mother's problem? Her thoughts jumbled and her belly hurt worse.

"Sorry. I didn't know," he said.

"It's just, things get better and then, all of sudden, they're bad again. It wears on a person, you know?"

He nodded.

"You think it's still that problem? From me being born? After all these years?"

"Whatever it is, it ain't your fault, Meg. Some folks just ain't strong. Ain't no one's fault. Not theirs, not no one's."

She watched the place where the moonlight on the straw changed to shadow. They listened to the stirrings of the barn. An owl wailed from a rafter.

"The Senecas used to say a person's mind goes weak when they ain't allowed to follow their dreams," he said.

Her mother had taught school and played piano before she had children and quit.

"I guess that's true for my mom."

He took hold of her hand to stand her up. "You should get home, so they don't worry."

She hoped he'd put his arms around her, but he guided her instead to the ladder. She climbed down reluctantly, then watched as his bare feet worked their way down the rungs after her. Scabs still showed at his waist. When he reached the foot of the ladder, she looked away, ashamed that Hank was Al's brother, ashamed that she hadn't told anyone. They walked past the sleeping livestock, to the barn door.

"I should go alone," she said, but he shook his head. "It could be bad for you if someone sees us," she added.

"Well, remember that next time before you come over."

The side of his mouth twitched, and for the first time she saw an anger he normally kept hidden. He laid his hands against the closed door. She pictured him toppling the entire barn over.

His brooding didn't bother her, though, something Greta could never understand.

"Guess I've been kind of selfish," she said.

He pushed away from the door and looked at her. "You're fine," he said. "Don't blame yourself for everything. Sorry about your mother."

She reined in the urge to touch him. They walked to the end of the driveway together, where he watched her cross the highway and get home, safe.

Chapter 7

Meg heard odd sounds from inside the saloon. She looked back to the Lee's driveway, where Arthur stood watching. Perhaps Charley was inside trying to rid himself of a drunken customer. Chances were the customer would forget her late arrival, and Charley could always be bribed. Lord knew she'd kept plenty of his secrets over the years.

Inside, Brandy moaned and grunted. Charley was kneeling next to the bar, disheveled, holding a lantern.

"Quick, Meg," he said. "Something's wrong. Get your Gramps."

"No." Meg turned away. "Arthur'll know what to do."

"He ain't in town—"

She was halfway out the door when she called out, not caring whom she woke, "He's back!"

Arthur was already settling in the loft when she reached the barn. He leaped down from the middle rungs of the ladder, a shirt in his hand. They ran side by side out of the barn, across the lawn and highway, him buttoning his shirt as he went. He could outrun her, but he slowed to her pace. She ran as quickly as she could. When they arrived at the saloon, she stopped just inside the door to catch her breath. He rushed straight to Brandy, not winded at all.

"Get a box!" Arthur said. "A big one. And towels."

"Charley, get the bar towels!" Meg called over her shoulder as she charged back out the saloon door. She dashed across the highway to her daddy's garage, where she knew she could find a box large enough for the pups.

The side door moaned, then stuck in its warped molding. She shoved harder, till it budged enough to give her a slim path into the garage. Wings flapped above her. She patted her way in the dark along a cement wall, past clutter shoved up against her great-granddaddy's milk wagon.

A narrow window lit Daddy's stack of crates and boxes at the back wall. She fumbled quickly, separating a dry cardboard box from a moldier one. Plenty big for Brandy's pups. She tipped it upside down and rat droppings fell out.

She hurried back along the side wall, but her foot caught in the rim of a metal milk jug. Daddy's collection worried her. Everyone knew holding scrap metal back from the war effort could cost a soldier's life. Please don't let Daddy's hoarding milk jugs bring anybody bad luck, she prayed.

She steadied herself at the door jamb, then forced the garage door shut. Clutching her box, she rushed back across the highway.

The first pup was already born. Several kerosene lamps dressed the bar, casting ample light on Brandy. The proud dame lay on a bar towel, licking jelly-like goo and blood off her wiggly blonde pup. Charley knelt beside them and cocked his head toward Arthur, who was washing his hands at the bar sink.

"Pulled him right out." Charley grinned, his gums showing. "Darnedest thing." He scratched his sparse head. It might've been the first time he'd ever paid Arthur a compliment.

The pup wiggled away from Brandy's tongue and latched onto a nipple. Arthur leaned over the bar to watch.

"See that?" Charley chuckled. "Hungry fella."

Arthur yawned. Meg smiled.

"How many, you think?" she asked.

"Feels like five more," Arthur said. "She sure was moaning, though. Hope none of 'em get stuck."

Suddenly Brandy grunted loudly. Her belly convulsed. The pup was shaken off her nipple.

"Grab him," Arthur said. Charley obeyed. "Here." Arthur tossed Charley a bar towel. "Set him in the box."

Meg helped Charley situate the puppy in the box with plenty of towels. Brandy grunted hard. Her belly spasmed violently each time.

"She sounds like Ol' Pete," Charley said.

"Something ain't right." Arthur was kneeling next to Brandy, pressing into her abdomen.

"What?" Meg asked.

Brandy yelped. Meg and Charley remained stooped next to the whelping box.

Arthur spoke softly. "C'mon, girl. You can do it."

They all watched, hoping a puppy would begin to appear. Brandy grunted and contorted, but nothing changed.

"Dang it." Arthur wiped his forehead into the upper part of his sleeve. Then he carefully slipped the fingers of one hand inside Brandy's swollen vagina. She squirmed at first, even growled some. But as Arthur's hand made its way farther inside her, she breathed through her nose, poised, as if she trusted him, painful as it was. Her eyes fixated at the towel beside her head.

"Good girl," he murmured. "I'm gettin' him, Brandy." Her belly lurched. "Hold still now, girl."

Arthur's hand began to reverse direction. He pulled so slowly, Meg wasn't sure at first. A tingle of dread ran through her. Minutes seemed to pass. Then his forearm tightened.

He shook his other hand toward Meg.

"Towel!"

She grabbed some clean ones from the whelping box.

"Sac's broke." He was pulling a wet tail and tiny paws from Brandy's birth canal. He wrapped a towel around them. Brandy's belly contracted. Then swoosh, the puppy slid out. Meg handed Arthur a dry towel which he wrapped around the pup. Brandy watched and panted, then gnawed on the cord and began to eat the afterbirth. But the puppy lay still.

"Gol dang it—"

Arthur picked up the lifeless pup and rubbed him vigorously in the towel. He stood and stepped back from Brandy, swinging the pup belly up, over his head, then down between his knees in an arc. He did it again, then checked the puppy's nose and mouth.

"Dang it!"

He swung the puppy again, then checked his mouth. A soft gurgle could be heard.

"Atta boy—" said Charley.

"C'mon, big guy." Arthur rubbed him roughly in the towel. "Wake up." He wiped the pup's nostrils and blew on his face. The puppy squirmed just slightly. Arthur rubbed and rubbed, as if summoning a genie from a magic lamp.

Meg stood beside them. "If you can wake up," she said, "we'll make you fat as Ol' Pete."

Arthur stopped rubbing and studied the pup's face. "We'll call you Li'l Pete, how'd you like that? Folks'll think you're one part hog."

Brandy moaned.

Charley tried to grin. "His ma swears he's pure pup, Art. She ain't been near no hogs."

"Keep rubbing and talking." Arthur handed the puppy to Meg. He stooped down to check Brandy. "Comin' head first. This one ain't stuck."

Meg carried the pup in her arms to a far corner of the saloon, away from Brandy's grunts, which were strong. The pup lay like a bean bag against her chest.

"After this one comes," Arthur said, "we'll see if Li'l Pete can eat."

Meg sang softly, "Hush, little baby, don't say a word…" Li'l Pete stirred in his towel. "Mama's gonna buy you a mockin' bird." Meg rubbed and cradled him. His closed eyes twitched.

"Lordy." Gramps had appeared with Gram at the top of the stairs. He was buttoning his overalls on his way down the steps, which creaked under his weight. Gram vanished back into the flat. Brandy gave a loud grunt, then snorted.

"Good girl," Arthur said.

The hard-working mama gnawed the bloody sac of her squirming third pup.

"Get her a drink, Charley, for cryin' out loud," Gramps harrumphed. He perched himself on a bar stool. "How many ya got so far?"

"Three, we hope," Charley said, setting a pan of water near Brandy, who now chewed an umbilical cord.

"Arthur, you can keep little Petey if it lives."

"Aw, that's all right," Arthur said.

"He's yours, if you want him. Hell, I mighta lost Brandy if you hadn't come."

Gram waddled down the stairs, carrying more clean towels. Meg brought Li'l Pete to her.

"Sure hope he makes it," Meg said.

Gram poked the puppy. "He's got a chance, honey, 'specially with you kids around. Keep rubbin'."

"Can't accept, Charley," Arthur said. "He'd bring you a heap of dough for sure. Pure breeds is hard to find these days."

"Just say thanks, Arthur," Gram said. "If Charley wants to give it, you take it." She headed straight to the whelping box with her towels. "Did it eat?"

"No'm, not yet." Arthur's eyes glazed over. "And yes'm. About the other." He pointed at Brandy. "Meg? Bring Li'l Pete over here? Thanks. Set him there, up against his ma, and let's see what he does."

Meg laid the puppy against Brandy's belly like a rag doll. Brandy licked him a few times, but she soon lost interest and lapped the water dish instead.

"C'mon, big boy," Meg said.

"Stick him right on there." Gram braced her hand on Meg's shoulder and wrestled herself down onto the floor. When she reached for the pup, Meg moved out of her way.

"C'mon you. Suck." Gram poked her finger in the pup's mouth and tried to attach it to Brandy's nipple. "Let's get at it." Li'l Pete's mouth pursed but then relaxed.

"That's the idea." Gram tickled the skin near Brandy's nipple to make it harden. Then she stuck her finger in Li'l Pete's mouth again. "Let's go. We ain't got all night." The puppy suckled three times, then stopped.

"That's right. Get your breakfast. Look, Meg, he's doing it." Gram tickled his mouth, and he sucked again. She kept after him. Every time he stopped, she tickled both him and his mother.

"Well, that's enough," she said finally, raising her arms. "It might take you three men to stand me up."

Gramps, Charley, and Arthur scurried to Gram and helped her back onto her feet. "Bring them other pups over before she labors again. They'll be hungry." Gram padded toward the stairs. "You come on up, now, Meg. School starts bright and early."

"Oh, gee, Gram. Please can I stay up just a little longer?" Meg licked her lips and hoped for a hint of capitulation.

"You'll be tired as all get out," Gram said. "It's the first day."

"Oh, Gram, please? I'm not working tomorrow. I'll get to bed early. And I'll do the dishes every night without you asking. Oh, please?" She noticed Gramps' and Arthur's smirks and had to join in.

"A whinin' woman usually wins," Charley said.

"I b'lieve one late night won't ruin her whole senior year," Gramps ventured. He winked at his wife.

"Outnumbered, am I?" Gram sighed. "Them pups is cute, to be sure." She turned back to head upstairs. "Oh, well, I suppose."

"Thanks, Gram," Meg said.

Gram stuck out her hand and wiggled her fingers without looking back. Gramps winked at Meg and followed his wife up to the flat.

"Three more, girl," Arthur told Brandy, offering her sips of water. She nursed her first and third pups while Li'l Pete snoozed, limp, in between them.

From outside, the sound of a truck could be heard pulling off the road onto gravel in front of the saloon.

"See if it's locked!" came a familiar male voice. When the door banged open, Al Wickham and two of his friends ambled in, red-faced. Fred Deckler and Clayt Palmer, boys who'd yanked Meg's ponytail in second grade, slouched against the wall.

"Saw the light," Al said. "How 'bout a bottle of whiskey? I got dough." He waved a ten-dollar bill.

"Go home, boys," Charley said. "We ain't open."

"Yer light's on, yer open," Al slurred. "How 'bout some hootch? Last day of summer 'n' all." Al snickered through his nose and looked to his friends, who laughed and nodded.

"Yeah, give us some hootch, or we'll take one of them pups when you're not lookin'. How many ya got?" Fred Deckler's knees almost buckled under him when he laughed. Al caught him under his arm.

"Get on out," Charley said, "or I'll call the sheriff. You ain't legal age. Out." Charley walked behind the bar and waited.

"How bout a shot o' whiskey, then?" Al asked. "Each?"

Charley took his rifle out from behind the bar and set it on the counter. Fred Deckler and Clayt Palmer eyed each other and began to inch toward the door.

"Aw, swell," Al said, standing in the center of the room. "You'd give a drink to the damn Indian, Charley. Damn coward won't even defend his country."

Meg glanced at Arthur. His jaw was clenched, and

he scratched slowly behind Brandy's ear.

"Get out now," Charley said, "and I won't tell the sheriff." He walked out from behind the bar.

Brandy's panting had changed to grunts. Arthur and Meg picked up all three pups and moved them to the whelping box, away from their mother's contractions.

"'Tain't patriotic, what you're doin' there." Al shifted his feet and stared at Arthur.

"Git," Charley told him. "Most likely you won't remember none of this come morning."

Al sneered.

"What's all the ruckus?" Gramps demanded from the top of the stairs.

Deckler and Palmer slunk out the door. Al backed up too, then eased himself out after them.

"Nothin, Gramps," Charley said. "Everything's fine."

Arthur and Meg knelt together next to Brandy, whose grunts came quicker now.

Chapter 8

By five a.m. the sixth pup was nursing and wagging his tail while Brandy snored. The siblings purred in their whelping box like a swarm of bees, overlapping each other in black and blonde heaps. All except for Li'l Pete, who lay inside Arthur's shirt like a lumpy potato.

"I'm gettin' some shuteye, kids." Charley yawned. "You best do the same." He lumbered toward his back room. "Turn off them lamps when you leave, would ya?"

Meg and Arthur sat on bar stools, watching the lump in Arthur's shirt. Footsteps clomped overhead. Within minutes the aroma of bacon grease drifted down the stairs.

"Cows should get milked," Arthur said.

"Gram's pancakes are delicious. The cows can wait a little, can't they?"

Half-moon creases appeared at the corners of Arthur's mouth. He'd never been to the upstairs flat before. Meg slipped off her stool and darted upstairs to ask permission.

Gram was standing at the stove, jiggling a skillet of eggs, one hand on her hip. A frayed apron was slung over the front of her bathrobe. Her heels splayed over the backs of hard-soled slippers, a sign of too much weight for her petite feet.

"How's the little one?"

"Fine," Meg said. "Might it be all right if Arthur comes up for breakfast?"

Gram arched her eyebrow, which meant the answer was bound to be "no."

"Gram, if you could've seen—"

Meg stopped herself. Surely it'd be the worst possible manners to send Arthur home hungry after such a night. She clasped her hands behind her back and waited. Gram set great store in good manners. The two women watched each other. Finally Gram shook her head.

"Bring him up. Bring that pup, too. Don't leave it alone, not if you want it to live. Don't leave that up to Charley, neither."

Meg raced downstairs.

"Quick! No accidents at the breakfast table!" She set two cloth napkins on the bar and held her hands out for Li'l Pete. "I'll diaper him so he won't make a mess." She waited for Arthur to unbutton the lower half of his shirt. Then she pulled the drowsy puppy out and set him on the napkins.

"We'll tie these on, just in case."

The napkins dwarfed the pup's belly. Arthur said nothing. He held his shirt open so she could lay the pup next to his warm skin. Li'l Pete snuggled his nose into his navel. Arthur's stomach muscles reacted to the tickle. They both laughed. Then Arthur cupped his hands around the pup while she fastened his shirt buttons as slowly as she possibly could.

The evening had left him with the scent of wet hay, or of her brother after a game of ball in the rain. She noticed the creases at the corners of his mouth again.

Sometimes his shyness seemed like an act, as if he tried to shield her from the grown man he was inside.

"My grandmother used to tell me a story," he said. "A boy saved his dog from a fire. He spit on his hands and rubbed it. And it got well. The dog's name was Beautiful Ears."

Meg nodded and reached up to straighten his ponytail. The thick strands stayed where she put them. "We can call him Li'l Pete Beautiful Ears. I like it."

Upstairs Gramps sat at the far end of the kitchen table, slathering butter on his toast. Gram stood by the stove, coffeepot in hand.

"Here's mud, Arthur. Help you stay awake." She poured a cupful at the place setting nearest Gramps. Arthur pointed to the pup in his shirt, then sat down next to Gramps.

"Did it eat again?" Gram asked.

"No'm. Not yet."

"Well, you best fortify it with some goat milk. Brandy don't seem much interested."

"He knows, Mother," Gramps said. "Let's don't boss him first thing he shows up for breakfast."

Gram blushed. "Just trying to help is all." She turned back to a burner on the stove and pretended to adjust the heat.

"Smells good," Arthur said.

"Dig in." Gram dabbed her forehead with a corner of her apron. "There's more of everything."

The Lees' rooster crowed. Meg seated herself across from Arthur and observed the way he sandwiched fried eggs between pancakes, syrup, and slices of bacon. She sipped her coffee to a rhythm of Gramps' dentures and Arthur's fork. Arthur leaned forward slightly, resting one hand on Li'l Pete each time he chewed. Gram hovered with her hands folded across her abdomen, proof she approved of the rate at which food disappeared from Arthur's plate.

"That was quite a night's work you put in there, Arthur," Gramps said, a dab of syrup on his chin. "You're a natural vet'rinary. Guess you know that."

"Thank you, sir." Arthur set his fork down and sat up straight.

"Could be a future in that, don't you think?" Gram asked, topping off his cup.

"This coffee's good. Thank you. Well'm—and sir—me and school don't seem to mix good. Sure would like to have my own farm, though. One day. Mr. Lee thinks I could."

"Farming might not be what it's been." Gramps frowned at a wedge of pancake on his plate.

Arthur glanced across the table at Meg. Her legs were crossed, and she allowed her dangling foot to shake.

"Don't discourage him, Father," Gram said.

"We've seen hard times, is all. Seen a peck o' change we never expected." Gramps wiped his chin with his napkin, then blew his nose in it. Gram bustled at the stove.

Meg stretched her foot farther under the table, away from Gramps, in search of Arthur's shoe. Without slumping noticeably, she tapped the table's center leg, then found the hunk of stiff leather. Arthur's eyes were black as shoe polish. He lowered his head to stifle a grin, and ate.

"You young folks finish up now." Gram ran the faucet while she wiped the counter. "Bus'll be over to

Greta's soon. Don't let me hear you fell asleep in class, missy."

****

"Wake up, we're here." Greta's face materialized like a ghost.

Exhaust spewed in through the window. The school bus was idling in front of Watkins Glen High.

"Oh!"

"Your eyes were twitching." Greta patted Meg's shoulder. "Hurry up. Karl Brewster's kinda cute all of a sudden. C'mon."

Outside the bus a cluster of senior girls in shirtwaists and saddle shoes waved.

"I need to wash my face," Meg said. "Tell everybody I'll see them at lunch."

She passed a display case in the main corridor with photographs of soldiers in uniform, former students who had already died in the war. Meg knew each face, but one picture startled her. Saturday's date was printed on a photo of Joe Ames, a close friend of her brother Ron. She pressed her hand to the glass. Joe had tried to kiss her once, on a Fourth of July. She hadn't noticed the announcement in the newspaper over the weekend. Each week it was getting harder to look.

Daddy's milk jugs continually haunted her. Were they bringing bad luck? Maybe Arthur would help her sneak them into his truck and haul them away to the army depot one night. It wouldn't be right, but it wasn't right to keep them, either. Every time she asked, Daddy changed the subject or left the room. Why couldn't he let go of things?

Mrs. B's classroom was located at the top of the stairs, next to the girls' restroom. Meg leaned inside the open door and found her former teacher writing on the blackboard.

"Hi ya, Mrs. B."

"Well, hello, senior! Excited?"

"Sure." Meg draped herself against the door jamb.

"Any help you need," Mrs. B offered, "you know, you just ask. College essay, you name it, Mr. B and I are happy to help."

"Thanks. That's so nice." Meg stopped herself from mentioning money.

"Something on your mind?"

"I just don't know what I want to be, is all."

What was the point of college when she knew she'd never be a doctor or lawyer?

"I could be a teacher, I guess. Maybe when June finishes her training. I don't see there's any rush, though." Having skipped two grades, she couldn't imagine teaching at twenty and being mistaken for one of the students.

"Besides, waitressing is easy. I can remember orders easy, the swell customers. And I add checks in my head. The cash register comes out to the penny. Everyone says."

"College isn't exactly job training, Meg. It opens up the world for you. You could do it."

"My Gramps says Ben Franklin didn't go to college."

"Fair enough. But he was a man. I think you'd love it."

A great yawn overcame Meg. Mrs. B laughed.

"Oh, gosh, Ms. B! Our bartender's dog had puppies last night." She yawned again. "Excuse me! Golly, what if I do that in Mr. B's class? He'll get such a bad impression."

"Just tell him first thing. He's soft about puppies. So'm I."

"So'm I." They both laughed. Meg reached out and hugged her favorite teacher.

"Let's talk again soon, Meg."

Several students strolled in through the door. The first day of senior year had commenced.

Chapter 9

Autumn's cool, dry days sent Meg and Greta rushing into the barn after school and up the ladder to the loft. There they'd find Arthur asleep with Li'l Pete tucked inside his shirt. The girls silently crawled beside them, their bare legs itching in the straw. Peals of giggles let Arthur know it was time for him to get back to work. But before long, Greta's sensitivities to grass, horse dander, owl feathers, and everything organic forced her to retreat to the house.

Then Meg would find herself alone with Li'l Pete.

The trees flushed early and were bare by mid-October. Meg treasured her secluded afternoons of homework in the airy loft, in the company of a rambunctious pup who loved to lie on his back and flaunt his round belly.

With Halloween approaching, the high school prepared for its annual masquerade ball, a welcome distraction for everyone from the war updates on the radio.

One afternoon Greta announced to Arthur, "You're taking us to the dance."

"Huh?"

Meg had tried to dissuade her all day but declined to give her reason. That was Arthur's secret, and she couldn't divulge it.

"We'll dress up as *Wizard of Oz* people," Greta

told Arthur, who lay stretched on the hay in the barn loft, barely awake from his nap. Greta arranged her skirt and sat cross-legged beside him. "You've seen the movie, of course?" He slowly shook his head.

Meg lay on her stomach and stared at the newspaper she'd borrowed from Mrs. B. Arthur would have to manage this on his own, which wouldn't be easy, considering what Mrs. Lee termed "Greta's German decisiveness."

"Meg and Li'l Pete will be Dorothy and Toto. I'll be Glinda, so I can wear my grandma's wedding dress. And you'll be the Scarecrow. The nicest guy in the movie. We'll stuff your shirt and pants with straw."

"I ain't in school," he said. "They only let students into dances."

"Mr. B said you can come. I asked." Greta opened a copy of her childhood *Oz* book and showed him a picture of the Scarecrow. "Meg's got the night off from Chef's. And, Frank Baum's mother-in-law was an honorary Mohawk. Isn't that something!"

Arthur surveyed the page. "Who's Frank Baum?"

"Oh, my." Greta shut her eyes. Arthur glanced at Meg, who smirked. "Frank Baum wrote *The Wizard of Oz*, silly."

Meg was trying not to laugh. Greta tapped Meg's saddle shoe with the toe of her own.

"His wife went to Cornell, by the way," Greta added. "Did you know that?"

Meg shook her head and let a giggle escape. "Didn't know that."

Greta had recently joined Mr. and Mrs. B's efforts to push Meg to apply to Cornell. Greta often said that she'd apply to Cornell herself if she had grades like

Meg's, but she planned to study music at Ithaca College instead. Meg admired Greta's lack of envy. She couldn't help feeling envious herself, much of the time. She would gladly have traded her grades for Greta's sturdy finances and lovely home.

"Wasn't Frank Baum mean to the Iroquois?" Meg asked. "Didn't Mrs. B teach us that? After Wounded Knee?" A dove cooed from a rafter.

"I don't remember. You're not helping." Greta tried to hand the book to Arthur. "I'll paint your face myself, Art. We all know you can dance. You have to come. Here, take the book."

"My hands're dirty."

"It's okay. Choo! It's old. Has chocolate stains. Choo! Take it." Greta's kitten-like sneezes were taking hold. "Choo! You can wear my father's work shirt. That one with patches. Choo! Oh, darn." Her sneezing spell accelerated. "S'cuse me. Choo!" In a minute she had disappeared down the ladder and out of the barn.

The dove cooed again. Ol' Pete grunted from below.

Arthur closed the book and crawled next to Meg, lying on his stomach, propped up by his elbows, his hair and skin ashen with dust from harvesting corn. He scooped up Li'l Pete and flipped onto his back. His shoulder sank into the straw next to Meg's. She smoothed the front of her bulky sweater.

"I can't dress up like no scarecrow," he said.

Li'l Pete sat on his chest and panted. Meg conjured up the memory of Arthur's firm grip when he spun her at the square dance just months before. He could dance better than anyone. She listened to the sounds of scampering mice and scratched behind Li'l Pete's ears.

"Folks at the feed store lost their nephew yesterday," he said.

"Oh, no. Not Doug?"

He nodded.

General MacArthur had mounted an attack in the Phillippines on the island of Leyte. The casualties were running high.

Doug, a gangly boy, used to help Arthur carry sacks to his truck. Meg and Greta loved to ride along, buy an apple, and giggle about Doug's hair, bright as an orange lollipop.

Gone? How could he just be gone? Meg's stomach went hollow. She tried not to think of her brother. Often at night she fussed in her bed, unable to sleep. She pictured Ron lifeless in the snow. Why couldn't this war end? Why was it taking so long?

"I could do two, three times what most of those guys do over there." Arthur's shoulder sank deeper in the straw next to hers while he stared at the rafters above.

She'd noticed a restlessness in him lately, and also in the other men who were still at home, except for Gramps and Daddy. The boys at school had it. And Mr. B, too.

"What would your grandmother do without you?"

"I'd come back."

"You can't know that. And anyway, you grow the food. For the soldiers and us."

"I know." He turned toward her, onto his side, and set Pete between them. "I'd need my grandma's blessing. Otherwise it's bad luck."

The air was chillier. Pete licked Arthur's chin. He shooed him off and moved away from her just a little, but he must have seen her disappointment because he leaned forward and pressed his lips against hers. She recalled the taste of salt water at the Jersey shore with Greta's family when she was ten.

"I'll walk you home." He coaxed Li'l Pete inside his shirt.

Outside, the sky beyond the lake was a backdrop of violet, burnt orange, and rose. The silhouettes of trees reached upward like skeleton fingers.

"It's strange, the fighting so far away from home," Meg said.

"My grandma says that's the way with white man's wars. They spoil other folks' land."

****

When Meg arrived in the flat, the aroma of beans, beef, and onion drew her into the kitchen. Two V-mails waited at her place setting on the table. She'd seen Ron's V-mails at Daddy's house before, but never received one herself.

"Take some privacy." Gram nodded, stirring her pot of chili. "Tell your gramps supper'll be a few more minutes."

After relaying Gram's message, Meg dashed to her room and closed the door. She smoothed each letter flat against her bedspread. Ron's swift black printing dominated the page. Hank's neat blue cursive was smudged in spots.

She wished the mail could arrive one at a time, instead of in batches. She'd save Hank's for last and read Ron's first.

Did Hank still like her? Should she tell Arthur he'd written her? Her palms grew clammy. She fumbled at Ron's letter, pulling apart the edges to make a flat page.

Hopefully Ron's allergies hadn't stuck him with a nasty cold.

Dear Megsy, I don't know what to write. The German shells fall so close sometimes, I swet more than I've ever swetted in my life. Which means my feet ain't never dry. French people are swell. Don't let folks tell you diffrent. They are worth fighting for. But don't show this to Mom. I know she takes it hard. I miss you. Keep up your studies. What a worthless bore is war. Love, Ron.

She read it again. He sounded fine, except for that last sentence. She would send him more socks. At least that was something definite she could do. Of course it wasn't helpful for him to know Mom had been worrying and made herself sick again. Meg wished she could quit worrying herself. Would she be like Mom one day? If only she could have Greta's unrelenting and comforting faith.

But didn't every mother and daughter pray the same prayer for their sons and brothers? Which prayers would God answer and which ones would be ignored?

She picked up Hank's V-mail and settled back onto her pillow. His tiny cursive barely filled the page. She pictured his knuckles squeezing hard on a pen, the same knuckles that hugged his cigarette that day in August. Her lips and tongue went dry.

Meg, I think of you often. How is school going? I do expect valedictorian for you, you know. Don't let a poor, hard-working soldier down! We've seen some mean action over here, worse than I could've imagined. It's the fatigue and the thirst that get you the most. We drink water you wouldn't subject your livestock to. At night especially, it feels like we're so far away. The wounded call out and there's nothing you can do for them. Well, that's as much as I can say that will get past the censors. Please write me if you can and tell me all the news from home. Yours, Hank.

She folded the V-mails in squares and tucked them deep inside her pillowcase.

It would be impossible to do homework tonight. Not now. Better to wake up early and race through the math, then read on the bus. *The Red Badge of Courage* would surely keep her awake all night if she read it after supper. She walked to the bathroom to wash her hands, but she'd lost her appetite for food.

Chapter 10

The gymnasium glowed like a giant jack-o-lantern that Saturday night when Arthur dropped the girls off at the Halloween dance. He'd volunteered to drive them and planned to sleep in his truck while he waited. Also, he'd be on call to take Li'l Pete if necessary, whom he claimed would tire out long before the girls.

Other late arrivals, witches and royalty alike, strolled up to the front of the school. Greta wiggled out of the truck cab first, taking care with the lace of her grandmother's wedding dress. Arthur hopped out and met Meg at her door to help with Pete. She handed him over, then pressed her parachuting skirt flat when she jumped down to the sidewalk.

"Sure you want to take him?" His cartoon expression meant he already knew the answer.

"If I can't dance with the Scarecrow, it wouldn't be fair to deny me Toto, too." She knew if it were daytime, she'd surely see his blush.

"Without Pete," Greta added, "it's hard to tell Meg's Dorothy. You could still come in, you know. Costumes aren't absolutely required."

His hands went up in self-defense. "I been up since four this morning, you two. Hope you win."

He hoisted himself into the passenger's side, pulling the door shut with a thud. Meg saw his thick blanket flap briefly, then disappear. She knew he'd be asleep soon, even as the band struck up "Don't Sit Under the Apple Tree (With Anyone Else But Me)."

"Boo, Glinda and Dorothy! And Toto, too!" Two boys covered in bed sheets passed by on the sidewalk.

"Who do you think that was?" Greta whispered.

Meg shrugged as she pictured herself dancing with Arthur alone here on the sidewalk, away from everyone else. She tugged gently on Li'l Pete's leash. "C'mon, Petey, time to go."

"I hope Karl Brewster asks me to dance." Greta looped her train over her arm. "If he does, meet me in the restroom by Mrs. B's room at 8:30. For hair and lipstick. All right?"

"Sure."

"I don't want to get called up on stage with a frizz mop and a chalk kisser. Can't abide that."

Greta's natural prettiness transcended her unruly hair and pallor, but Meg could never convince her of it.

"8:30."

Near the school entrance, a cluster of boys dressed as pirates lingered by the shrubbery. Al Wickham, with a tri-cornered hat, black wig, and fake beard, ogled the girls with one bloodshot eye, his other hidden behind a black eye patch.

"Ahoy, lassies."

"Too drunk to get in," Greta whispered.

"'I'll get your little dog, my pretty.'" Al snickered. His friends laughed and surveyed the girls from the shoulders downward. Meg folded her arm across her chest and tightened up on Pete's leash.

"Heard from my brother yet?" Al called out.

Meg glanced at Greta, who continued walking. "Just ignore him," Meg whispered. She hadn't told anyone about Hank's V-mail. Goose bumps prickled her bare legs.

"I may just write Hank and say I saw you out with the injun's dog," Al called after her. "Get 'im riled so he'll kill some Krauts finally. Make a hero out of him yet."

Outside the entrance to the gym, Mr. and Mrs. B stood stationed at the refreshment stand.

Relieved to see them, Meg called out, "Oh, Mr. B, you look so young!" then she clamped her hand over her mouth. Mrs. B laughed. Having shaved, Mr. B looked dimpled and prom-ready in his black tuxedo. His teeth were more square-shaped than Meg remembered.

"Can't be FDR with a beard."

"Cute, isn't he?" Mrs. B patted his cheek. Her sequined gown hugged her curves in just the right places.

Meg, eager for an excuse not to enter the dance, offered to assist them. Li'l Pete could sleep under the table, she suggested, concealed by the white tablecloth. And when Greta spotted Karl Brewster through the gymnasium doors, Meg urged her to fill up her dance card for the night. The band even launched into "Over the Rainbow."

"Dorothy doesn't dance?" Mr. B peered over the tops of his glasses, handing Meg a glass of punch.

"Not tonight." She tasted the blend of cider, peaches, and grapes. "Mm." She lifted the edge of the tablecloth with her saddle shoe to see Li'l Pete settling down to sleep. "We could watch him, if that's your concern," Mr. B said.

"Gee, thanks. I think I'm just tired." Adults were

always pressing her to spend more time with people her own age, when sometimes she just preferred the company of adults. She turned to Mrs. B. "Besides, Greta and I were talking about Frank Baum's mother-in-law—"

"Matilda Joslyn Gage!" Mrs. B gasped and launched into a familiar jag about early American women's rights activists, her favorite topic and one that Meg enjoyed hearing even if she'd heard most parts of it repeated more than once.

"Baum's wife—" Mr. B interjected to Meg when his wife paused for a breath, "She went to Cornell, you know."

Meg laughed politely. "Oh, my." There it was, again. Cornell.

"Those ladies were smart cookies." Mr. B winked at his wife.

"Ben! You compare them to baked goods!" Mrs. B positioned herself against the edge of the refreshment table, her Eleanor Roosevelt gown shimmering in the outdoor lamplight. "Now, dear. More care with how you put things!"

Before long, Mrs. B's spiel had ranged from the veto powers of Iroquois women to their marital habits and the invention of bloomers.

"Those Seneca squaws were sensible. No corsets for them."

"Very civilized," answered Mr. B, handing his wife a glass of punch. "Well said, dear."

Meg smiled, noticing an energetic and affectionate blend of sarcasm and admiration in Mr. B's eye.

Through the gym door Meg surveyed the array of dancing couples. An acrobat with a hobo, a princess with a cowboy, a priest and a gypsy. Just the same, groups of girls leaned in clusters against the wall, sans partners. Meg felt a tinge of gloom tug her.

If women could suddenly have veto power now, she thought, could we veto the war? Couldn't there be another way to stop Hitler?

****

At 8:30 Meg excused herself and carried Li'l Pete to the upstairs restroom near Mrs. B's classroom. Inside "the Ladies'," two students were sharing the mirrors over the sinks. One, dressed as an angel, dabbed rouge on her powdered skin. The other, dressed as Little Bo Peep, wore high heels and washed her hands with Ivory soap. Her bleached hair hung loosely, as did her shirtwaist, as though she'd chosen the wrong size dress. When she glanced up into the mirror, Meg had to mask her surprise. Jessie Mae Burke, Hank's former girlfriend, the belle of Watkins Glen High School, appeared a haggard version of herself.

The three girls looked at each other via Jessie Mae's reflection in the mirror. Meg recognized the angel as Annette, Jessie's best friend.

With Li'l Pete wiggling in her arms, Meg forced herself to speak. "Hello, Jessie. Hi ya, Annette."

Jessie Mae shook water droplets off her hands into the sink, still watching Meg. She seemed older than her seventeen years. Her lips were thin, and her exquisite eyes had dulled somehow. Meg blushed, aware of her own crooked pigtails and the bobby sock that had sunk into her shoe. Why had Hank taken a sudden interest in her last summer? Why had he abandoned this womanly girl so recklessly?

"Cute dog," Jessie Mae said.

Just then the restroom door swung open and Greta entered, corralling her wide skirt into the room. "Oh."

Li'l Pete barked.

"Hush, Pete," Meg said.

Jessie Mae gave a soft laugh and patted her hands dry on her Bo Peep apron.

"Don't worry." Jessie's voice echoed a rich tone within the tiled walls. "It's all yours." She glanced at Annette. "Let's go."

They passed Greta and pushed the door open. The sounds of their heels faded. Meg set Li'l Pete on the floor and traced a floor tile with the edge of her saddle shoe.

"I feel terrible."

"Why? You didn't do anything." Greta parked her pocketbook on the sink and sprinkled water on her curls. "You should know something. There's a rumor going around." She turned to look directly at Meg.

"What?" Meg felt her stomach knot up.

"There's talk Jessie Mae saw that woman in Corning. In August. And whatever she got from her—some kind of tea, I guess—it didn't agree with her. She has Hank to thank for that, not you."

"What woman in Corning?"

Greta sighed like an older sister. "I don't always tell you things because you're younger, but you should know. Hank could've married her before he left. Instead of telling her to get rid of it. Some girls die from this kind of thing. Like Jean Harlow."

"Jean Harlow died of kidney failure, didn't she?"

Greta sighed again. "You have to quit being so naive. I bet your Gram thinks I stay in the barn with you and Arthur. You think she'd let you come over every day if she knew what really goes on?"

"Nothing goes on." Meg's face burned. "Honest." How could Greta even think it?

"Boys have one thing on their minds, and Arthur's no different. If they don't act on it, after a while they make themselves sick. That's what I hear, anyway. You be careful. And read that book I lent you."

Meg had hidden Mrs. Sanger's *What Every Girl Should Know* at the bottom of her underwear drawer, where it still lay unopened.

"That woman in Corning isn't a doctor," Greta added as she traced her lips with a red lipstick. "Hank shoulda known that's where Jessie'd go. I hear Mrs. B's trying to get her to see a real doctor, but Jessie's afraid her parents'll find out."

Meg leaned her cheek against the cool tiled wall. Arthur's warmth had often caused a stir in her, making her legs into jelly and her mind furry and vague. Was that how Jessie'd felt about Hank?

"Do you think Hank knows she's gotten poorly?"

Greta shrugged. "Have you heard from him?"

Meg nodded, then wished she hadn't.

"What'd he say?"

"Nothing much."

"I never thought of Jessie as fast." Greta blotted her lips on a white hankie. "She sure was the prettiest. It's a lesson for all of us."

Soft dribbling sounded in the corner of the restroom. A yellow puddle gathered on the floor under Li'l Pete. Then he squatted and pooped.

"Aw, Pete." Meg grabbed some tissue from a stall. Li'l Pete panted and wagged his tail. While Meg cleaned up the floor, Greta unhooked a window to let the odor out. The band was playing "Stardust," a song Meg had just practiced on the Lees' piano earlier that afternoon.

"If he messes on stage, I'll never recover," Greta said, handing Meg another wad of tissue.

At the sink, Meg bent over to wash her hands, but the Ivory soap slipped away and onto the floor. It slithered like a fish when she tried to retrieve it. "I think I might skip the costume parade, if you don't mind."

Greta touched Meg's shoulder with cool fingers. "Don't worry, I'm sure you can handle Arthur." They glanced at each other in the mirror. "And Hank's a million miles away."

****

Once outside, Meg set Li'l Pete on the ground and patted her leg for him to heel. The stars were sharp as ice crystals. She hesitated before saying her usual prayers for Ron and Hank. Instead she asked for help for Jessie Mae. And of course for her mother.

What if stars were the hearts of ancestors? Folks who'd been caring in life, like Gram and Aunt Lizzy. And then after they died they watched over their great-great-grandchildren when they called out for help. Great Aunt May might be up there. Arthur's grandmother might be one day, too.

If Meg's own mother had known how to end a pregnancy, would she have done it? Then Meg might never have been born. But then maybe her mother could have been happy.

When she reached the truck, Li'l Pete barked before she could stop him. Arthur sat up in the truck cab with a jerk.

"Sorry." Meg reached for the door handle. Arthur

waved a sleepy hand. "Sorry to wake you."

He pulled his heavy blanket to him and yawned. "I'm awake."

Chapter 11

"Then I bet Greta thinks I'm a bastard," Arthur muttered after Meg confessed what was on her mind. Li'l Pete lay in his lap, paws and legs tangled, limp amid the spokes of the truck's steering wheel. "She'd be right, too. Though my grandma don't see it like that."

He explained in a matter-of-fact way that for the Senecas, all births were legitimate, whether parents of a child were married or not. A girl's family always welcomed a baby in the Seneca world. And birth control was talked about and occurred in different forms. His grandmother knew remedies that could keep a girl safe if a girl wasn't ready to raise a child.

"Don't you ever go to no stranger," he told Meg. His eyes were dark and moist in the starlight. "You ask my grandma if you ever need help."

His words were sensible, not embarrassing at all. Why was talking with him about such things easier than talking to Greta? She relaxed her hand in his fist so he might loosen his grip. Then she threaded her fingers through his.

She hadn't told him about Hank's V-mail yet. They never spoke about Hank anyway. She still wondered if he'd seen Hank's car that day in August outside her parents' house. Arthur kept secrets better than anyone, so she never knew what he knew unless she asked.

A layer of cloud began to cover the moon out the truck window while the band played a faint, unfamiliar tune.

It didn't seem right to say nothing about the V-mail, but she'd never really liked Hank in the first place. She'd just felt flattered by his attentions, was all. And now she guessed he had used her to make people think he didn't care about Jessie Mae. Maybe he was even trying to fool himself. A soldier far from home had to put his faith in something. Maybe that was why he convinced himself that he really liked Meg. But she couldn't return the feeling, especially now.

Arthur's ribs rose and fell against her arm while Li'l Pete snored muffled barks from a romping dream.

"Chasin' squirrels," Arthur whispered.

Meg nodded and leaned her head on his shoulder, inhaling the rosemary sprig in his breast pocket, deciding not to mention Hank.

****

Later that night, wind rattled the loose pane in her bedroom window. Her pillowcase felt like Arthur's cool denim. It was as if his fingers still grazed her cheek, with their tortoise skin and caress like Gram's, firm but gentle, stroking her hair during childhood fevers.

Arthur had kissed her only once in the truck, then pulled away. She would have liked more. That sweet, lurking urge persisted as she flipped from her back to her stomach to her side in bed. Was this how Jessie Mae had felt about Hank? She sat up and switched on the lamp on her table.

Inside the top drawer was a diary Ron had given her several Christmases ago, still blank. She could draft a letter to Hank, then copy it later onto a proper V-mail.

She could explain about Arthur, as well as her concerns about Jessie Mae.

Her pen raced across the page. But when she reread what she'd written, she scribbled it out. A soldier needed comfort from home, not a "Dear John" letter. The radio announced daily reminders that letters must encourage boys abroad to stay alive and bolster their spirits. The folks who transferred the letters to microfilm would black out anything else anyway. And as much as she wanted to ask Hank to write to Jessie Mae, to let him know how sad she looked, every way she wrote it just came out mean and meddlesome. She wrote two more versions, then gave up and shut off the light.

Dear Hank, Good to hear from you. School is fine. Senior year is much easier than last year, though I'm not sure why. Maybe the teachers want us to remember them fondly as we prepare to embark from the "nest." By the way, Charley's Brandy had pups in September. The runt we named Li'l Pete after Mr. Lee's hog. He is so cute. Gets himself into all kinds of mischief now. I am told I am too lenient and should discipline him more. But I can't even scold him, because he wags his tail as if to say, "Look what I did!" I just returned from the Halloween dance where Greta and I were Glinda and Dorothy, respectively, from The Wizard of Oz. Li'l Pete was Toto, of course. Be well. Come home safe. Meg.

****

As November's cold descended on the lake, farmers posted requests at the feed store for extra help harvesting corn. Arthur and Mr. Lee pitched in, having finished their own haul early. Li'l Pete, now a spunky ten-week-old, traveled with Arthur to the farms to romp free, and herd calves and sheep, who paid him little mind.

Meg accepted more hours at Chef's after school, where she could scratch out math solutions between taking orders and serving hot meals to families and women from the army depot. Arthur and Mr. Lee would stop by for coffee at the end of their day before giving her a lift home.

To free up the passenger seat, Arthur and Li'l Pete would jump into Mr. Lee's truck bed, leaving behind a clean towel for Meg to sit on, protection from their muddy residue. Mr. Lee hardly spoke when he drove. So Meg looked forward to her solemn rides home with the sound of whistling through gaps in the truck's window molding. Arthur sat close behind her, against the outside of the metal cab, holding onto Pete, whose ears flapped in the wind at the same rate as his master's ponytail.

"He's livin' in the barn for good now," Arthur had told her. "Chewed the heck out of my grandma's sofa leg, and she says that's that."

Each night the chill in the air bit harder. Blackness had shut out the sunset by the time they deposited Meg in front of her folks' house. Mr. Lee and Arthur would let the engine idle while they watched Meg run across the highway to her grandparents' flat.

****

"Your teacher called," Gramps announced one evening. "Him and his wife had words with us about you."

"What about?" Meg shivered at the door, despite the warm smell of frying pork.

"Them grades o' yours." Gramps rattled his newspaper and cleared his throat. "Mother?" He called in the direction of the kitchen. "She's home!" He removed his glasses and motioned to the far end of the sofa for Meg to sit down.

She couldn't imagine what grades he referred to. Everything was an A, as far as she knew. Except possibly phys ed class, where she fumbled volleyballs with a unique degree of regularity.

Gram lumbered into the room, wiping her hands on her apron, then placed herself into her rocker, her arms pressing the armrests. "Did you tell her, Father?"

He shook his head. "Waitin' for you."

Meg sat forward on the sofa, scouring her memory for a failed quiz or forgotten homework assignment. Had she forgotten to write her name on a test?

"Mr. B spoke to us about your grades, honey." Gram folded her hands across her abdomen. "He says he's never seen the likes of them before." She rocked back, and the chair groaned.

"They're concerned, Meggy." Gramps coughed. "They say they can't abide a girl with your abilities passing up a chance to go to college. They say you're at the top of your class." He frowned.

Meg sank back into the sofa and closed her eyes. Never before had she spoken to her grandparents about college. After all, neither of them had gotten past eighth grade. She rarely discussed school with them at all.

"There's a New York State scholarship, they tell us," Gram said. "Hank Wickham had it, apparently. But since he won't be using it any time soon, they think you can most likely get it. For Cornell, honey. Think of that!" She beamed with all her teeth exposed, something she rarely allowed to happen, due to a gap in the upper palate.

"Well." Meg sat forward again and took a breath to collect her words. "I heard that scholarship wouldn't pay for half Cornell's tuition, Gram. And I don't know what I want to be, you see. It just seems impractical, since I don't care to go to law school or medical school."

Gram glanced at her husband. "That's what they said she'd say."

Gramps harrumphed. "Why don't you want to go to medical school, if you got the talent?"

"Well." Why would her teachers trouble her grandparents with something they knew nothing about? Why didn't they speak directly to her? "I guess I'm too squeamish for doctoring. And I'd worry about making mistakes on live people. As for the law, I think I'd end up just fighting a lot of bad laws and getting myself into a peck of trouble."

Gram shook her head. "They must have other things at a place like Cornell, honey. All them books you read? Don't they have anything for that?"

Meg pictured herself spending hours in the library at Cornell with its lush carpet and crammed stacks of dusty books, while her sisters labored at the army depot, resenting her. Her grandparents just didn't understand. College was a costly luxury she had no business considering.

"I don't know, Gram."

Gramps rocked forward and back, then swept himself up to standing. "I ain't so sure about a young girl moving to Ithaca all by herself, anyway. Your teachers seem to think they know better about this business than we do. But I ain't so sure. Wish I was expert on such things." He stomped off in the direction of the bathroom.

Meg stared at the floor, listening to the stove sizzle in the kitchen.

Gram fanned her fingers in the air. "If you got the talent, you got to find a way to use it. Your poor mother had the talent." She sighed mightily. "Don't fret about particulars. Things can sort themselves out." She pressed her hands on the chair's arms to boost herself to standing. "Come help me with them chops."

"That state scholarship's not enough, Gram."

"Mm-hm."

Meg watched her grandmother tuck a loose wisp inside her bun and waddle off toward the kitchen.

What went on inside that gray-haired head sometimes sure was a mystery.

Chapter 12

Early Thanksgiving morning, flurries gusted across the lake. Meg stared out the kitchen window as she dusted a rolling pin with a handful of flour. Snow spread lace-like across the hillside; black trees and tilting cattails created a random pattern on the white.

Weeks of icy weather had frozen parts of Seneca for the first time in years. Gram's tall tale of ice skating from Valois to Watkins as a young girl suddenly seemed credible.

Every Thanksgiving morning since she'd turned nine, Meg had risen early to bake pies in dusky solitude. This year she laid crusts in two pie tins destined for Aunt Lizzie's, where she and her grandparents would feast on roast turkey that afternoon. A third pie she planned to run across the street to her parents and sisters, as peach pie was her mother's favorite. And the last pie she'd save for Arthur, who'd offered to take her skating later that night to christen the ice.

The wind blew low notes through holes in the rafters while Meg dwelt on a V-mail that had arrived the previous day. She'd only read it twice, but Hank's words played over and over again in her head like a record on a phonograph with the arm raised, set to repeat.

Meg, Thanks for your letter. I can picture you as

an extra pretty Judy Garland. And Greta, obviously, was perfect as the good witch. There's a Jewish fellow in our company who, like me, doesn't sleep at night, so I showed him your letter. We smoke together, listen to the gunfire, and wait for the sun to come up. He sure is a swell fellow. I've never known anyone Jewish before. A French lady gave us both two new sets of socks. You've no idea how important dry feet are when you're far from home. Don't let anyone try to tell you war's thrilling or adventurous. It's the most wretched thing done by man. The guys say maybe this one will be the war to end all wars. I sure hope it's true. Work hard at your studies. Could you please send a picture? Hank

She rolled out several crusts, then poured herself a cup of coffee from the stove. Had she led him on in that V-mail she'd sent him? She surely hadn't meant to. She probably should have mentioned Arthur's name after all. By not saying anything was she inviting trouble?

A heavy gust landed against the kitchen window and whistled through the eaves. She flipped on the radio in time to hear that the weather in Europe was freezing, also. She imagined Hank and Ron trudging through the French countryside in the snow.

****

The wind beat against her when she crossed the highway to deliver her parents' pie. She held it to her chest, swaddled in a dish towel, stomping her boots so as not to slip on patches of ice. To get out of the wind, she headed for the back door, passing between the house and garage, past the outhouse, which hardly stank at all in the cold. Viv was waiting for her in the kitchen with fingers to her mouth in a "sh-sh."

"They both have colds," Viv whispered, pointing

upstairs.

Meg hovered just inside the door, trying not to seem disappointed. She would've liked to see her mother's face when she smelled the warm pie. "Where's June?"

"Working. Time and a half, holiday pay."

The kitchen was silent, dark, and reeked of cat litter. "Aren't you cooking?"

Viv shrugged. "I'll do a chicken tonight. You off to Aunt Lizzie's?"

Meg nodded.

"What are you doing after?" Viv asked.

"Skating. With Greta." Meg would've like to invite Viv to join them, but she knew Viv wouldn't want to be seen with Arthur. "Wish Mom and Daddy Happy Thanksgiving for me." Stepping back into the cold, she tugged her collar over her cheeks.

"Will do. Same to Gram and, you know, all of 'em."

"Will do." Meg started toward the garage, then turned and waved for Viv to come lean out the door. "I'm borrowing Ron's skates."

Viv pursed her lips in a flat, sisterly frown, revealing premature jowls. "Who for?"

"Arthur."

"Stay close to shore," was all Viv said.

"Will do."

Inside Daddy's garage, wind rattled the rafters. The milk wagon stood like frozen livestock. Meg gazed ahead, stepping over clutter, avoiding glimpses of the hoarded scrap metal that should've been turned in.

Ron's hockey skates hung, tied together by their laces, on a nail at the front wall by an oxen yoke. They were coated with dust and a sticky veil of cobwebs. With the help of a cloth from the oil can shelf, she wiped them clean.

A year ago, Ron had given her new skates for Christmas; genuine white leather, with black heels and silver blades. All her life she'd skated in hand-me-downs, so the rigid new leather hurt her ankles at first. She'd even cringed inside when her sisters saw them, knowing they'd think such a gift extravagant. But Greta had received new skates for Christmas too, so after many visits to the Watkins rink, both girls' skates were gray and broken in and no longer drew attention to themselves.

Meg slung Ron's skates over her shoulder and pictured his wide bare feet inside them. He never wore socks when he played hockey. Socks slowed him down, he always said.

Maybe, with luck, a French grandmother would invite him inside today and let him sit by her fire and dry his feet. Or offer him a slice of pie or pastry. Hopefully someone in his company was watching his back, just as he had always watched hers when they were children.

She pressed his skates against her chest and noticed the leather's faint salt smell. Then she hurried back out into the weather, ignoring the milk wagon, and never once setting eyes on Daddy's hoarded metal jugs, so as not to invite bad luck.

****

It was seven o'clock that night when Meg dashed into her bedroom to change into her skating clothes. Gram had trailed behind her while Gramps finished parking the truck behind the saloon.

"Them ski pants is in the trunk," Gram had said.

Meg wrestled with the snap on the hand-me-downs. She wished she'd turned down that second slice of Aunt Lizzy's pumpkin pie, which now made the waistline awfully tight. How was it possible Gram had once squeezed into these narrow woolens when she was Meg's age?

"Be back by ten." Gramps was huffing, catching his breath at the top of the stairs. "Stay close to shore," he said. "That ice is new."

Meg grabbed Gram's heavy plaid coat from the living room closet. "I will. Don't worry." She slung her skates over one shoulder and Ron's over the other.

"We do worry." Gram emerged from the kitchen. She handed Gramps a cup of tea.

But Meg blew a kiss off her mittened hand and whisked herself out the door before they had time to say any more.

****

The sky was a silent, black dome specked with glitter and shredded clouds. Arthur stood at the top of the road that led downhill to the lake. His hands were thrust inside his pants pockets. Li'l Pete ran back and forth, sniffing dried weeds in the snow. Meg guessed Arthur'd been watching from the upper barn window for Gramps' truck to arrive back from Aunt Lizzie's. His leather collar was turned up under his loose hair. He shrugged his shoulders and shook his head, as if to send stray hairs away from his mouth and eyes.

"Happy Harvest Festival," she told him, rising on her toes to give him a quick kiss on the lips. The taste of his toothpaste made her wish she'd brushed her teeth, too. She felt the warm breath from his nose.

"Pumpkin pie, hey?"

They giggled.

"I saved you one of my apples. The crusts came out just right this year." She draped Ron's skates over his shoulder while Li'l Pete pranced in circles around their boots. When he pawed her leg, she reached down to scratch him behind the ears. "Where's Greta?"

"Ate too much, is what she said. I think she thinks it's too cold out." He winked. "You aim to catch me when I fall?"

"It's easy, really." They crossed their arms behind each other's back, hugging the waist to set up resistance against the sloped, icy road. "It's like dancing except you cut into the ice with your blades."

Li'l Pete trotted along beside them but slipped on his bottom. He scrambled to stand, but all four legs slid out again and he lay splayed on his belly on the road. Arthur laughed and picked him up and carried him on his hip.

"Let's go, big fella. If we fall and crack the lake, she'll get mad, you know, and swallow us whole." He shook his hair again and looked over at Meg. "Then we'll turn into lake trout. If you catch us one day, you might eat us for supper and not know it."

From out of the fields below, a pickup truck bumped and skidded onto the road, flashing its lights and weaving back and forth up the hill. Arthur and Meg quickly jogged out of the way, into the snowy field. Laughter squealed from the back of Al Wickham's pickup. The horn honked again and again.

"Out of the road, Injun! This ain't your country! Chicken liver deadbeat!"

An empty beer bottle flew out from the back of the

flatbed. Arthur ducked in time for it to miss his head. Li'l Pete snarled and barked as the truck swerved on the ice, then shifted to a lower gear and lumbered to the top of the hill.

Meg wanted to hurl the bottle back but knew she'd never hit the truck. Ron could've aimed that beer bottle at the cab and hit it for sure. She wished she'd tried harder when he'd shown her how to throw straight.

But Arthur just stared at the ground. She wanted to shake him.

"You never fight back, do you?"

He set Li'l Pete down on the snow. She heard the truck screech onto the highway as it turned the corner at the top of the road. Arthur's eyes were glassy but still.

"No. I don't."

He straightened and watched her till she blushed. Then he turned away and walked down the hill toward the lake. She followed, as his words settled on her, and Li'l Pete bounded in her footprints in the snow.

****

Seneca lay hushed by a thin layer of powder, scalloped by the morning's wind. Meg and Arthur found a log to sit on while they laced their skates. Li'l Pete scampered nearby, sneezing into the snow, donning white whiskers. Meg wrenched her laces, knowing skate leather stretches, wanting to secure as much support for her ankles as possible.

She listened to the absence of lapping waves and seagull caws. This frozen lady seemed the bitter sister of the lake she loved, whose waves always rolled with a lullaby, peopled with duck families, insects, and bobbing seaweed.

Meg glanced at Arthur. It was as if he were

somewhere else; still beside her but far away from the lake or Valois or lacing up skates. She recognized something she'd seen in her Daddy at times: a staunch willpower, which she didn't understand or agree with. But maybe it wasn't hers to understand.

"Here." She knelt in the snow and undid his frayed laces. "They need to be snug." Her fingers ached as she yanked on the strings. Li'l Pete tried to bite one lace and pull it with his teeth, but she gently pushed him away. "No, Pete." Arthur reached down and scratched behind his ears.

"Good boy," he said.

They held hands when they hobbled toward the ice. "Just glide," she told him. "Use your leg muscles, keep your ankles straight."

He bent forward at the waist at first, like most novice skaters. Li'l Pete tiptoed behind him, balanced lightly on all fours.

"Do this!" Meg spun in a wide circle and slowed to a stop. When she looked back, Arthur and Li'l Pete stood with their legs angled out like tripods, watching her, their heads tilted in the same direction.

Arthur took one step toward her on the ice, then held up his hand. They heard a low, quiet creak like a loose board in the barn loft.

"Ain't set yet."

Li'l Pete romped back to shore. He wagged his tail and barked.

Seneca was the deepest of the Finger Lakes. Where exactly was that abrupt drop-off? Here at the bend? Meg slid one foot gently toward shore. But the lake groaned.

Cracked webs splintered through the ice and the

lake gave way. A memory flashed. Of sinking into cold, light-filtered depths. And going to sleep. She'd fallen in the lake once as a baby, she'd been told, and was afraid of the lake till she learned how to swim. She'd always imagined drowning as falling asleep. Could it be that simple? A drowsiness setting in from below the water's skin?

Arthur lunged toward her, but their skates broke into ankle-deep water. Their blades slid on rocks, then sank into sand. They grabbed each other's wrists and laughed.

"She only swallowed our feet," Arthur said. "Glad we missed that drop-off."

They gripped each other's elbows and trounced the ice several yards back to shore. The icy water sent shivers up Meg's legs.

"Gramps'll have a fit if I come home wet."

Arthur pulled her up onto shore, then up against his body. His lips pressed on hers, smooth and warm. When she ran out of breath, she pushed him away just slightly, then replaced the kiss. He kissed her back, hard. After a while, he parted his lips, just barely, to take in more air, which she tried also. Then their open lips folded inside each other's till his tongue met hers.

She felt dizzy and clutched his coat to keep from slipping, balanced on her skate blades on the stony shore. This was a different kind of a kiss, mysterious and inventive. She copied the way he swallowed when he paused to take a breath.

His legs were splayed out for support and to match her in height. They pressed against each other, his pelvic bone against hers. And she pressed back in response. Until she realized it wasn't his pelvic bone after all.

A chilly breeze began to blow. Li'l Pete barked.

"We should go," Arthur said.

His hair tickled her cheeks. She tried to disengage—not willingly, though. When she finally pulled away, she reached back for his hands to help steady her skates on the stones.

"I think my feet froze," he said.

"Well, the rest of you sure didn't."

His teeth shone in the dark as they made their way back to the log to change to their boots. When they sat down, he shook his head.

"I sure can't guess what you mean by that, Meg."

First she hit him on the shoulder, harder than she intended. Then she laid her head against his arm. He cupped his hand around her waist.

"I could kiss you all night," she said.

"Me, too." He gently moved away and began to change out of his skates. "Which is why we best get you home."

Chapter 13

The weeks sped toward Christmas with preparations for final exams and the Nativity pageant at Valois Church. Meg and Greta squeezed in daily rehearsals after school, scheduled around Meg's waitressing hours. Sometimes Arthur would join the rehearsals, turning pages for Meg at the piano while Greta played harmony at the organ.

When Arthur picked Meg up from work in his truck, he'd hum the Christmas hymns slightly off key, which made her giggle. He hovered in her thoughts all the time now, whenever she worked or studied or practiced, like a sprite too shy for the light.

During music rehearsals, Meg sometimes thought of Ron and pictured him stopping off in a country church where an organist practiced these same hymns, only with lyrics written in French or German. She thought of Hank, too, but never for long. Now that Jessie Mae was well again, few folks mentioned Hank's name. Meg wished for his safety, but that was all.

She'd become caught up in Mr. and Mrs. B's enthusiasm about Cornell. Of course the expense was still impossible. But she found herself stealing time to develop an essay for a scholarship application, due in early January. Mrs. B had often talked about the value of a liberal arts education.

"It can widen your perspective," she'd said.

"There's a whole world out there beyond Watkins and Valois."

Meg decided not to mention the essay to Arthur. Why hurt his feelings, seeing as he'd quit school and most likely wouldn't go back? And besides, she most likely wasn't going to Cornell anyway. Writing the essay was simply an exercise. Cornell was for rich kids like Hank or Greta, not somebody like Meg.

****

The first morning after semester finals, a voice on the radio ranted at full volume from the kitchen.

"Harsh weather in Europe is hurting the Allies but helping Hitler!"

Meg sat down quietly at the breakfast table, where Gramps frowned into his coffee. She resisted an urge to pour herself a cup, so as not to disturb him. Gram padded into the kitchen, too, and sat down. Sam followed and purred at Gram's feet.

The newscaster described a battle in a forest in Belgium where the Americans were suffering major casualties. With the U.S. Air Force grounded due to bad weather, Hitler was advancing fast.

"Coffee, honey?" Gram whispered.

"I'll get it," Meg whispered back. "Want some?"

Gram shook her head. Gramps stared at the radio. They both looked paler than usual. Meg knew they worried about Ron, but she pictured him alert, crouched in a trench, as if he were deer hunting. He'd always been a good shot.

"Why don't you two go back to bed? I'll get breakfast. I've got the lunch shift, so I'll catch that late bus. I've got loads of time."

"Have a seat, honey," Gram said.

"Confusion is running rampant," the announcer warned. "Hitler's Nazi commandos have infiltrated Allied lines. They dress in uniforms stolen off our fallen soldiers."

The announcer detailed how the commandos, who spoke perfect English, were causing havoc by switching road signs, cutting telephone wires, and spreading false rumors among Allied troops. In response, Americans were interrogating every occupant of every vehicle in the area by asking them trivia questions.

A local female announcer continued the broadcast from Watkins.

"It's a good thing our boys studied their state capitals back in grade school, folks. And without giving too much away over these air waves, be glad your sons know such particulars as the object of a certain Mouse's affections."

"What's that mean?" Gramps harrumphed.

"Minnie Mouse," Meg said. "The cartoon?" Gramps shook his head. "If you'd come to a movie sometime, Gramps—"

He stood up, his eyes glazed. "Our boys got to kick them Krauts to Kingdom Come, by God. I got no time for some nonsense about a mouse!"

Gram slumped forward in her chair. Long hairs strayed from her bun. Meg noticed a tear on her grandmother's cheek, quickly brushed away.

"There's something you should know," Gram began.

Later that afternoon at Chef's, Meg shook back tears and leaned on the counter to top off Arthur's coffee. Bing Crosby sang "I'll Be Home for Christmas" over the radio.

"Gol-lee, not again," she said. "They play it every half hour, I swear."

Gram had told her that morning that Ron was missing in action. The Red Cross had notified her parents days ago, but Gram had insisted she would wait to tell Meg when her finals were over.

"'Twasn't right, not to tell you," Gram had said, holding Sam tight in her lap. "But your teachers want that valedictorian prize for you. And I know you deserve it."

Meg mulled over Gram's choice as she stared out the diner's grand window. Of course it was the best decision. She might've failed her exams if she'd known. She glanced at Arthur, who sat at the counter and stared out the window, too. Decorated with tinsel and red glass balls, the window framed a violet sunset. Thick snowflakes fell.

Arthur had known about Ron for days, even while Gram kept the news a secret. When he arrived at the diner and Meg told him she'd found out, he didn't say he was sorry. He just nodded and watched her in his silent way.

What good would it have done if Gram had told her sooner? It wouldn't have brought Ron home. She dreaded the evening's Christmas pageant, where people were bound to tell her how sorry they were.

Maybe Ron had been captured and was living in a prison camp. He took orders well. He could keep his head down and stay alive, in spite of the Germans.

"You got to do as you're told," he'd often told her. "Don't challenge people and make waves. Don't ask teachers too many questions. And listen to Viv, cuz she's the oldest. Life's easier if you stay outa trouble."

Or maybe he had escaped and was hiding in the woods. Soldiers were coming home missing toes from frostbite and gangrene, or worse. What if he was hurt? Or sick? Questions without answers hammered her thoughts all afternoon. In some ways, she wished she still didn't know he was missing.

"Number ten."

She turned to grab three loaded plates from Mike, the short-order cook. She welcomed the work. Cleaning, scraping plates, wiping counters, mopping the bathroom. Anything with a purpose. Anything to stay busy and not think.

After she refilled drink orders, she tried to top off Arthur's coffee again. But he covered his cup. A few drops hit his hand.

"Sorry!"

He wiped his hand on his overalls and shook his head at the cloth she offered him. "Don't they ration here?"

"Oh." Suddenly she understood. Arthur was troubled about Ron in more than one way, she knew. And here she was lavishing coffee on him in public.

But she was glad Arthur hadn't gone off to war, that he was needed on the farm. Sure, America needed more young men to volunteer, especially boys as capable as Arthur. But she couldn't see the sense in losing him, too.

The door opened, letting in a blast of cold air and setting bells on the door handle jingling. Al Wickham propped the door open for a soldier on crutches. Meg studied the wan face and shaven head, then recognized him as Matt Palmer, Hank Wickham's best friend.

Palmer swung himself between his crutches on one

leg. The other leg was amputated just above the knee, his pant leg tied up in a knot. The end flapped when he moved.

"Table for two." Al Wickham shut the door. His nose was pink from the cold. Neither Al nor Palmer looked at Arthur.

Palmer reached out to shake Meg's hand. "Sorry to hear about Ron." His voice was deeper than she remembered.

Al stood close to Arthur without looking at him, bumping against the back of his swivel stool as if he wasn't there.

"Guess you heard about Hank?" Al kept his eyes steady on Meg's. She smelled alcohol on his breath. "Cuz if you didn't, you should know. Seein' as he writes you and what not."

Meg's stomach clenched. "What?" Another local boy dead, MIA, disabled?

Palmer touched her shoulder.

"He's not dead. Don't worry."

Meg glanced at Arthur, who stared into his coffee. She wished she'd told him about Hank's V-mails. Why had she hidden that from him? She saw the skin on his neck grow dark.

"Guess not any of us know what we'll do till we do it." Palmer sighed. "Can't ever tell ahead of time which guys are the cowards."

"Hell, Matt. Hank ain't yellow. He didn't run any sooner than them other guys, that's how I heard it." Al's face flushed. "Them Krauts was gunning all them prisoners. It's fair to run then, ain't it? I don't call that cowardly. Not like chicken folk who don't even sign up."

Arthur didn't flinch.

"Where is he?" Meg asked.

"I dunno. He was in a hospital in France, I think." Palmer adjusted his crutches. "He kept talking to his dead buddy."

"Some Jew from his unit," Al said.

"The Krauts rounded up the whole company. Tried to gun them all down. Hank's one of the lucky ones. He'll get a psychiatric discharge."

"Not if my old man can help it." Al stood tall, shrugging his shoulders, a gesture Meg recognized as one of Hank's.

"Maybe he lost his marbles," Palmer said evenly. "But maybe he can get 'em back."

"Sure. He'll get 'em back, all right." Al looked down at Palmer's crutches and blushed. Then he peered over at Meg. "Too bad for you, though. Hank sure liked you. Guess you two ain't the match made in heaven after all, like he hoped. What with his marbles gone and your mother. That'd be the weakness coming from both sides."

Arthur stood up abruptly and reached for Al's collar, but Palmer had already shoved Al out of the way.

"Calm down, Injun," Palmer said. Then he turned to Al. "Don't you know when to shut up?"

"Hey, he's the coward. Not my brother." Al unzipped his jacket and dropped it on the floor. "Too chicken to sign up, and then he tries to steal Hank's girl. We know what you're after. Stinkin farmhand—"

Meg's face was hot. She took hold of Arthur's arm. His muscles tensed.

"Y'oughta be in jail, Injun. Ain't you nineteen?

How old are you, Meg? Does he even know? He flunked so many times, can he count?"

Sixteen, she thought, but said nothing.

Arthur's hands were fists. She could hear his breath as if he'd been running. Palmer backed up on his crutches and stuck one out in front of Al. The diner quieted as Arthur stepped away from Meg toward the door, his arms loose at his sides, his eyes steady.

"Just gonna run away like you always do?" Al said. "Stinkin' coward." Al looked around the diner with a grin. "This'un's for Hank," he announced. He seemed to hesitate, then suddenly lunged at Arthur, using full force. With a swift, light movement, Arthur stepped aside, missing the punch and sending Al into a tumble, which knocked his chin hard on a tabletop and sent him face down on the floor. A few customers snickered.

"Nice going, Wickham," said Palmer.

As Al picked himself up, Mike, the short-order cook, slipped from behind the counter and grabbed Al's arms. Rose, the night waitress, positioned herself between Al and Arthur.

"No fighting here, fellas," she said, her voice low.

Al tried to wrench himself away from Mike, but couldn't. Blood oozed from his nose. He peered at Meg and mumbled, "What kinda American are you, lettin' him touch you? Wouldn't let my brother, a real soldier. But you let this coward?"

Meg's throat locked. Arthur stood still, with his eyes fixed on the floor.

"Time for you to move along," Rose said, handing Al his jacket while the cook steered him to the door. Al stopped to wipe blood on his sleeve, then looked hard at Meg. In his eyes she saw a twisted hate.

"Out the front," Rose added. "Now!"

Mike, the cook, grabbed Al's elbow and sent him outside into the night.

"I'll seat the soldier," Rose told Meg, barely glancing at Arthur. "Take your friend out the back." Running her fingers through her permed gray hair, she told Palmer, "Follow me. Best seat in the house for you, soldier."

Chapter 14

Arthur never did appear that night to turn hymnal pages for Meg at Valois Church. Gram filled in for him instead, balancing her girth beside Meg on the narrow piano bench. The evening passed like a scene in a Christmas globe, as if Meg watched from outside the glass while the contents settled in slow motion.

She longed for Arthur beside her but saw that as the war wore on, folks resented him more and more. She missed Ron and wished the pageant would end so she could rush outside, where her toes and ears would sting at first and then grow numb. She wanted to stop feeling anything.

Who would love her if Ron was gone? Of course there was Gram, but Gram was getting on. Meg had always counted on Ron as her lifelong ally. She'd pictured him at her wedding one day. Their children would play together as favorite cousins, creating a secret pact kept private from Viv's and June's kids.

"I'll come home soon," she told her grandparents after the concert with Greta hovering nearby as a decoy. Meg needed to see Arthur. The truck ride from the diner had been silent.

"Don't be late," Gramps said. "I don't reckon I'll be too cheerful comin' back out in this cold to getcha."

The barn's windows were dark, but Meg guessed Arthur was in there. She and Greta hugged each other tight. There was nothing to say. She watched Greta trudge toward the Lees' house.

Snow clouds masked the stars, as if angels knew where Ron was but wouldn't tell. The barn door groaned when she opened it.

Straw cushioned the sound of her footsteps but Ol' Pete stirred in his pen. She heard the sound of straw rustling up in the loft. Li'l Pete greeted her from the top of the ladder, panting and wagging his tail in circles. She climbed up to the loft.

Arthur lay on his back under a heavy blanket, one arm folded under his head. In the dim light she could see his eyes were open. She patted Li'l Pete's head, then crawled on her knees to kneel beside Arthur.

"How was the music?" he asked.

"Fine." She sat back on her haunches and looked out the window at the pale gray night. When she looked back at Arthur, she noticed the light tinted his face blue. "I should've told you about Hank's letters. I'm sorry."

He watched her with blue-black eyes.

"I didn't want to be mean and not write him back," she added. "Guess I made a mess of it."

He blinked once, but his face was serene. He seemed older. "Maybe you should do. Maybe you should like him."

Li'l Pete nudged Meg's elbow, then tried to crawl onto her lap, but she held her hand up for him to stop. Arthur reached his hand out from under his blanket.

"Come 'ere," he said, and Li'l Pete scooted over to lie beside him so Arthur could stroke his fur. "Hank could help you, maybe. Once he gets better. Rich war hero like that."

"I don't like him, honest I don't."

Arthur just watched her and kept on petting Pete. She felt suddenly tired, and wanted to lie down but knew she shouldn't. She missed Ron, and wondered if she'd ever be able to ask his advice again. Was that selfish? She faced the window, willing tears away, focusing on flurries that squalled outside the window.

"Think Al's right about Mom?" She touched his hand. "What if I end up like her? I've got her knack for school, you know. What if I lose my marbles someday? You think my kids are destined to be crazy?"

He shook his head and turned her hand over, laying his palm on top of hers on the blanket.

"It don't have to work out like that." He sounded certain. "Maybe your mom's dream wish got smothered. That's how people get weak-minded. A person's got to hold onto their dream wish or they lose their way. You got to protect a dream."

It sounded too simple. Her mother had shown such promise as a girl. Gifted at school and music, she'd begun teaching as a young woman. Maybe marrying Daddy had been the mistake.

"Whatever desire you got way down deep, you got to take care of it," Arthur said. "Don't let nobody interfere with it. A mistake saddles a family with troubles for seven generations, that's how the old folks say it. They try everything to help a person get his dream back."

She loved his Seneca talk. It seemed practical, not guilt-inducing like the reverend and his sermons on sin.

What was her dream wish exactly? Was it going to Cornell? There had to be much more to it, though Cornell was definitely a piece. She wanted work that meant something, not just bussing tables. She didn't want to feel stuck here in Valois like her mother and sisters. The world held endless possibilities. But who could guarantee she'd ever find a home out there without getting lost? What if she failed? At least in Valois she knew what to expect.

She stroked the calluses on his fingers. Li'l Pete tried to lick both their hands, but when they ignored him, he stood and padded off to a corner of the loft, circled the straw and curled up to sleep. Meg slid next to Arthur on her side, on top of the blanket.

"I might sign up," he said.

"Don't. Mr. Lee needs you. Your grandma, too."

"They're running out of able-bodied men, Meg. Even if it ain't my country, technically, I should sign up."

He saw himself as foremost an Iroquois. She admired that.

"You're all your grandma's got. And Mr. Lee needs you. Who else could do all the work? Don't sign up." She couldn't stand to lose him. Ron was missing. She couldn't imagine losing Arthur, too.

"You should go home," he said.

She touched his hair and settled her face close to his.

"Ignore what Al said," she told him. "He's twisted."

He looked at her sideways, still lying on his back.

"Go home," he said.

She traced his eyebrow with her finger, then her lips. He smelled of sweet grass and sage. She pressed her lips on his. He kissed her back. She laid her arm over his shoulder, around his neck, and he pulled her to him, then up on top of him.

"Don't sign up," she whispered.

Her thick coat and his blanket separated them. As they kissed, Meg felt her worries step back into the dark corners of the barn.

After a while, the blanket slipped away. Meg fingered Arthur's ribs through his denim shirt. The fabric under his arm was damp. She felt herself sweat inside her coat, cold as it was in the loft. A button shaped like an acorn jabbed her in the breast more than once. Undoing her coat didn't seem like a good idea, but the acorn button jabbed her again and hurt. She reached for it, still kissing Arthur, undoing it and adjusting her coat. He pulled back and looked, then threaded his fingers through her hair with one hand and undid more of her buttons with his other. It wasn't what she meant to have happen, but a thrill went through her when his hand met her breast.

His way of kissing her sent her into a deep tunnel far away, or into a forest. Nothing seemed real. They observed each other with eyes at half-mast. His hand followed the outline of her back inside her open coat, then smoothed across her hips. She felt delicious and desperate and pressed against him. He reached between them and undid the button at his waist. But Meg stopped his hand.

"No?"

She shook her head. "We can't." Her head felt full of cotton. It was hard to think or form real thoughts.

"Why not?"

She noted a mixture of anger, willpower, and affection in his voice. In a vague way she sensed her period had started.

"We can't. Really."

He watched her for another moment, then kissed her on the forehead. He rolled over on top of her and pressed himself into a push-up. From there he hopped to standing and disappeared down the ladder. The kiss on the forehead had been more like a peck.

Could people make love when they had their period? She had no idea how it worked. Was she simply lucky? She could see now how Jessie Mae got into a fix.

She sat up on the blanket, on her knees, and waited. Would he come back? She heard Li'l Pete puppy-woof in his dream.

This was something Meg had only dreamed about, read about. But reading and dreaming paled. She ached for Arthur's scent, his arms and chest. His voice. His unshaven face.

She closed the buttons on her coat, trying to count the weeks since her last period. Only two since just before finals. Strange. Maybe she was exhausted from the late night studying. And of course the news of Ron. She needed to get home to change her clothes. Was Arthur coming back?

After a few more minutes, she heard his feet on the ladder. She sat up straight. When he reached the upper rungs, he leaned his arm on the loft floor.

"C'mon," he said. "I'll walk you home." He wore his leather jacket, his hair back in a ponytail.

She wondered where he'd gone.

Li'l Pete stirred, then barked.

"You stay, Pete," Arthur said. "He chewed up my grandma's husk dolls. He's really sleeping out here for good now."

Outside, the flurries had stopped and the sky hung

low. They held hands as they walked on the fresh powder. They could see their breath.

At the saloon, he kissed her briefly on the mouth. She reached out to kiss him again, but he diverted her with a hug, then turned away. After he'd taken some steps, he looked back.

"I love you," she told him.

"I love you, too." His voice was soft in the muted air. He turned, scanned the empty highway, then ran home.

Upstairs in the bathroom, Meg found no sign of her period. She leaned back against the wall and closed her eyes. For the longest time she imagined his scratchy chin on her neck and her body pressed against his.

Chapter 15

She didn't sleep that night. Shifting positions caused sudden wild tossing of the sheets. She'd never lain awake all night before, and here she was spending hour after hour thinking of nothing but the warmth of Arthur's skin. Tired but not sleepy, she watched the stars, waiting for them to fade. It was a slow vigil. She wondered if Arthur snored soundly in his grandma's cottage. Languid under a lumpy handmade afghan, his feet stretched out from underneath covered by woolen socks with moth holes and one large toe hole each. Meg flipped over onto her back for the umpteenth time, then gave up and swung her legs off the bed. Reaching into the dresser for paper and pen, she rearranged herself upright and tried to write. As Gram often said, if you can't sleep, might as well get up and do something useful.

Dear Cornell University Admissions Committee... It was hard to concentrate. Meg flopped onto her stomach and balanced herself on her elbows, the pad of paper in front, her knees bent behind. She laced her ankles together in the air, intertwined, twisting and rubbing. She pictured Arthur sleeping on his back with his mouth slightly open, as she'd seen many times when he nodded off in the barn loft while she worked on homework. His naps were always brief, accidental, light. Any significant movement would wake him with a start. "Didn't mean to fall asleep," he'd burble, exhausted from his four a.m. chores. "Guess I'm tuckered out," he'd apologize if he yawned. Gramp's word, *tuckered*. She scribbled it in the margin of her page next to the word *Dear* and added the letter *A*. *A tuckered Dear.* She drew feathered lines around it to frame it, loose, like his hair in a gust of wind when he didn't tie it back, when it smelled of hickory from the fire, or on special occasions when it smelled of soap. She squeezed her feet tighter together to help her focus on the essay. Why did she want to attend Cornell?

With a Cornell education, I feel I cannot fail to achieve great things.

What great things? What could she bring to the world? Sure she knew how to study and make high grades in school, but what did that have to do with a world at war? She stared out the window. The stars were bright as ever. She imagined Arthur next to her on the bed. The imagined scent of hay and cinnamon filled the room, lulling her into a quasi sleep.

In her demi-dream, she lay wrapped tightly in blankets next to Arthur with a two-foot-tall bundling board set between them, its length running from their armpits to their toes. Hours of soft sleep passed till Arthur abruptly wrangled free from his many blankets, grabbed the board, and threw it under the bed. He knelt over her, his silhouette like a shadow in the dim light as he began gently liberating her from her swaddling blankets. Then suddenly Li'l Pete barked, and someone opened the bedroom door.

Meg sat up with a start, finding herself alone in her room with eerie morning light. The door was shut, but her sheet and blankets lay tangled on the floor.

She dressed, then tiptoed downstairs and hurried across the road. She wanted to see Arthur. If he wasn't in the barn, she would tap on his bedroom window at the back of his grandmother's cottage. She needed to speak up for his staying home from the war.

But outside the barn, she found different sizes of fresh boot prints in the snow. By the door was a clump of chicken feathers. Who was in the barn? Was Mr. Lee back early from his business trip? She hesitated to go inside, till she saw the footprints led to the woods. Then she glanced toward Arthur's grandmother's cottage. Red paint smeared the white front door. As she crossed the yard, Arthur opened the door outward and waved.

"Couldn't wait to milk the cows for me, hey?" He was smiling.

She ran to him and pushed him aside, shutting the door for him to see the red paint. A white feather was stuck in the paint's thickness. She understood the chicken feathers' meaning.

Arthur stared at the feather quietly. His eyes focused within, and seemed to pass quickly from surprise to anger to something like acceptance only different.

"I ain't surprised," he said.

"There's an awful lot of boot prints by the barn—" Her words tumbled. "Are they yours? Is Mr. Lee back? Are some of them his, too?"

"No…" His face changed.

He started across the yard and then began to run, scanning the snow between the barn and the woods. Then he rushed inside. When she caught up with him, he was scaling the ladder to the loft. Quickly he leapt back down the ladder.

"What?" she said.

He guided her out of his way, his face weary and alarmed. When he ran out of the barn for the woods, she tried to keep pace with him.

"Arthur—"

The sound of his feet hitting the snow faded.

She followed him into the woods, elbowing branches which broke, leaving sticks scattered behind her. The footprints led in the direction of the swimming hole. She hadn't seen it since summer. It'd be iced over by now.

Her throat was raw when she finally heard the sound of the falls. Her belly tightened. Up ahead she could see the footprints stopped at the edge that led down into the gully. There was no sign of anyone. A chill ran through her at being alone in the woods. Never before had she been afraid of being alone in these woods. It was as if something had changed. The quiet she had always loved was different, strange somehow. She thought of Ron and wished he were here. She thought of him hiding in a wood in Europe, in Germany or France, with the never-ending possibility of Germans lurking in the shadows, watching him, waiting for their opportunity. She ran faster to reach the edge of the gully, to find Arthur, to escape the silence.

When she stopped at the gully's ridge, she saw Arthur struggling up the slope from the swimming hole, cradling a bundle in his arms. His face was racked, and dark spots smudged his leather jacket.

Li'l Pete's tail hung limp, askew under his arm. Below, on dented ice, Meg saw a wreath of blood.

"Go home!" He paused on the slope, shielding his bundle from her.

She moved closer, but Arthur heaved the bundle to his chest and turned away from her. Blood dotted the snow around him.

"How bad—?" she asked.

"Go home!" He sank to his knees on the snow and hunched forward.

She started down the slope. Surely he could save Pete. She'd seen him work a miracle with a wounded calf. She slowed her pace till she was several feet away from him. He set his jaw on his shoulder and choked out soft words.

"Ain't no use you seeing him like this."

"Hurry—let's take him—"

Arthur shook his head hard. Tears were streaming down his face. From his lap, blood pooled onto the snow. Meg looked past Arthur's shoulder and saw Pete's white skull was smashed. His eyes were open and his nose quivered. His front leg was twisted the wrong way around. But he barely whimpered.

"Can you—?"

Arthur shook his head and leaned his face close to Pete's. She stepped closer and could see Pete staring up into Arthur's eyes. His belly heaved.

"You have to let him go," she said.

Arthur crumpled forward in a low sob. She touched his shoulder, then looked away, down the slope, at the red circle of blood on the ice. Her tears were warm on her cheeks. She forced a breath and spoke.

"You have to."

After a moment, he wrenched his back till she heard the quiet crack.

Arthur's wail echoed through the gully.

She knelt and held him tightly in her arms,

knowing that in a fierce act of kindness, he'd snapped Pete's neck.

Chapter 16

They would choose a spot deep in the woods, high up the hill above Valois Cemetery, where no one would disturb him.

Meg was sure Al Wickham had done it. He'd been drunk at Chef's and probably drank more as the evening wore on. But they had no proof.

Arthur found a broken trough which he cleaned, then made a lid from split logs. Meg lined the trough with straw from the corner of the loft where Pete liked to sleep. Then she searched the barn for the knotted rag he liked to chew, the one he'd used for games of tug-o-war.

Arthur lifted Pete's body tenderly into the trough, setting his favorite ham bone near his paw. Meg tucked the rag under Pete's leg, but fixed her gaze off to the side so as not to remember him like this, damaged and limp.

The barn felt so vacant. Where was the wagging tail, the sniffing for mice, the mischievous nips on sleeves? Maybe Pete's spirit would be waiting for them on top of Cemetery Hill.

Low clouds dulled the morning sky as they trudged through the woods behind Meg's folks' house. A hint of chimney smoke scented the air. Arthur shouldered Pete's coffin, steadying it with one hand, carrying a pickaxe in his other. "Ground's frozen," he'd said.

Meg carried two shovels and watched for bits of holly and pine that she could braid into a wreath while Arthur broke ground. They followed a dirt road to a path along the edge of the cemetery, where they passed the cracked headstones of Civil War graves. A black iron cannon sat in the center of the hill, aimed at the lake, as if on guard for them. When they neared a cluster of pines, Meg pointed to a familiar plot with two granite stones standing together, layered with snow.

"There's Great Aunt May and Uncle Jim."

She had told him plenty of times how they'd cared for her when she was a baby, after her own mother couldn't take care of her anymore.

"Do you remember her, your aunt?" Arthur set his axe down and shifted the trough to his other shoulder, steadying himself against a heavy gust from the lake that rattled the tree branches.

"Just at the funeral."

Aunt May's face flashed in her mind, chalk white inside her open coffin. It was as if she'd died yesterday, not thirteen years ago. If only Meg could picture her alive.

She would train herself to remember Pete prancing in the snow or slipping on ice. Or nestling against her and Arthur in the hayloft.

Farther up the hill, the gravestones thinned until the cemetery merged into forest and what had been the Seneca burial ground. Arthur set his axe down and scanned the forest floor.

"Somewhere up here," he said.

Meg helped him set the trough near an oak tree whose girth boasted its age. He had told her once that local Senecas buried their elders here, near this oak.

She wandered in a circle, searching for more berries to weave into her wreath while Arthur broke up the ground with his axe. The thuds on frozen dirt silenced the birds and sent squirrels scampering to their burrows.

The walk uphill had warmed Meg, but now she felt the wind's chill. Threads of fog drifted into the forest like ground-level clouds. Then it happened quickly. The fog grew dense, masking the lake from view. Soon everything beyond the nearest trees disappeared into whiteness. She spread her arms and felt the dampness whisk through her.

"Angels," she whispered.

Sometimes she felt like she knew what death was, but then those moments would vanish just as quickly as they came. She knew it had something to do with having seen Aunt May in the coffin back when she was little. Meg had been so young, but even then she knew the scary life-size doll in the coffin wasn't her aunt. Aunt May herself was somewhere else.

Meg stood still in the silence and peered into the fog's whiteness. Her chest and shoulders relaxed. "He'll be in good company, Arthur."

Arthur wiped his eyes on his sleeve, then covered his face with his hand.

The icy dirt sounded like gravel as they dug their shovels into the ground. With each shovelful, she would glance at him. His hair and jacket fluttered against the pale backdrop of fog, but his face held still with grief, fixed on his task.

Finally he paused, as though he realized the hole was more than big enough.

"It'll fit now." She nodded softly.

But he backed away and braced his hand against a

tree.

She wanted to go to him and wrap her arms around his back, but she knelt instead and waited. She considered lifting the trough herself, to at least spare him that job. But if she slipped and dropped Pete— Her hand rested on the wooden lid. It was her silent farewell, silent except for the wind's low, sustained note as it blew through the trees.

Arthur coughed, then swung away from the tree. With his back to Meg, he cleared his nose, then wiped his face briskly with his sleeve.

"Let's do this," he said.

Together they lowered Pete into the grave. Kneeling forward, Meg tested the lid to make sure it was shut tight. She squeezed Arthur's hand.

Please keep the ants and worms away from Pete.

Arthur brushed a handful of dirt back into the hole with his free hand. "If anybody bothers him here," he said, "I'll kill 'em."

Chapter 17

That night, from inside her bedroom, Meg heard Gram's voice from the living room telling Gramps, "Hasn't hit her yet. Still numb from the shock."

So somehow they knew. But Meg couldn't talk about it. She brought *Now in November* to the kitchen table for meals, pretending to read but really just scanning the words. And they let her.

Every time Meg passed through the saloon on her way to work, Brandy's tail thumped the floor, bringing back memories of Li'l Pete's birth and how he almost didn't make it. How Charley gave him to Arthur as a kind of thanks for saving Brandy and her littlest pup.

Meg did feel numb. Some things were just too cruel to face. Her eyes stung whenever she heard Brandy's tail thump, but she kept moving, briskly, out the saloon door just in time to catch the bus for work. With careful timing, she could watch for the bus from the kitchen window, hurry down through the saloon to avoid talking to Charley, and wave to her sisters or Daddy from across the street before hopping on the bus. They seemed to be waving her over every time she saw them there in their front window, as if inviting her in. Meg figured they had probably heard about Li'l Pete and Arthur. But thankfully the bus was always there waiting. She wouldn't have to answer their questions, and they wouldn't see her cry.

With school on Christmas break, she rushed off daily to her long shifts at Chef's. The hungry shoppers and travelers kept her busy juggling orders for hot pie and hotter, fresher coffee, distracting her, protecting her from her own thoughts.

One day, some time toward five p.m., Rose waved Meg away from the cash register and into the kitchen, where Mike, the short order cook, was grilling steaks. The only customers left out front were a couple of recent widowers who had no family close by for dinner on Christmas Eve.

"I've got those two, honey. See if Mike needs help," Rose had said.

Meg pushed open the swinging door to a tidy kitchen and remarked, "You didn't leave me much to clean up, Mike."

Mike frowned as he flipped a couple of steaks onto plates, and quickly nodded toward the back of the kitchen. Then he headed out into the front with the steaks, without looking back.

Arthur was standing in the boot cove by the back door, his hands shoved deep into his jacket pockets, staring at the floor. Bits of melting snow disappeared in his loose hair. When Meg approached, he didn't look up.

"Hi, ya," she said.

As he stared at the floor, he spoke in a flat, quiet voice. "I have to go."

"But—"

He shook his head and closed his eyes as if interruptions might break the spell or ruin the truth of what he had to say.

"I think I might hurt someone if I stay here, Meg.

I'm going to sign up. Grandma gave me her blessing. Least this way if I hurt someone it's legal. If I drive to Buffalo tonight, I'll see my mother. I can leave the truck with her, too."

Meg wanted to argue. *Why now? The war's almost over. It won't make any of us proud to see you wounded or dead or crazy from shooting boys who happen to be German. Don't go.* But she couldn't speak; her throat was too tight. Greta would call her unpatriotic, but she didn't care. She saw nothing good in this war anymore. What was the sense of butchering so many young men on both sides? Finally her throat opened up enough to say, "Don't go."

He reached out his hands from his pockets and took hold of hers. She felt him press something cold, metallic into her palm.

"It's a bracelet my dad gave my mother. I thought maybe you could wear it. Maybe it'll bring me some luck."

She nodded and slipped the thin silver bracelet onto her wrist.

"You shouldn't go, you know," she said.

He bent and kissed her softly, then pulled away; but she opened her lips and drew him to her. She kissed him as deeply as she could to make him stay, to change his mind. After a moment he kissed her back, his arms full around her, as if they were in the barn together, as if they could kiss each other for hours. But then he stopped.

"Watch the stars at night," he said. "I'll watch 'em, too, so we can talk to each other. I'll always be there, Meg, every night."

He reached for her hand to kiss her palm, but she

grabbed the leather of his coat and pulled him tight against her, their cheeks pressed together, hard. She felt her tears mix with his in his loose hair, his scratchy jaw and soft lips on her throat.

"Come on, now," he said softly. "I best beat that storm tonight."

She heard the kitchen door swing open and felt him nod at someone, whose hands promptly gripped her elbows and held her, firm. It was Rose.

Meg gulped her cry like a child. She watched Arthur slip out the back door quickly, and felt the rush of cold air as Rose hugged her captive. They listened for the truck's motor to gun. The wheels spun on ice before the truck screeched off toward the lake and the highway. Rose loosened her grip saying, "I'm sorry, honey." Meg stepped toward the door and pressed her cheek flat against the icy window.

She felt as if time had stopped, as if she'd suddenly found herself trapped inside a strange void surrounded by layers of frosted glass. It wasn't so much that he'd gone off to war; she couldn't begin to fathom that yet. Maybe it was this new hollow space without him. But suddenly it was Li'l Pete, too. Why would anybody want to hurt a puppy? Why did God let that happen?

Now she couldn't run to the barn in the morning to give Arthur the Christmas scarf she'd knitted or watch him wear it while he worked. She wouldn't hear his low-pitched words or read his dusky eyes. Or feel his touch, his mouth. Or hold him when he spoke of Li'l Pete.

Even as Rose and Mike talked while they drove her home, and then while Gram and Gramps talked afterward, Meg's mind remained fixed on Arthur in his truck on the snowy highway, on the three-hour drive to Buffalo. And of Li'l Pete, in the cold ground above the cemetery.

Chapter 18

That night, the snow outside her window cast her room in silver gray. Vague images prickled her imagination, some willed and some not. Arthur's hair, his powerful brown shoulders, his back and buttocks as he floated in the gully last summer. Over and over again she tossed onto her side or stomach to stop her thoughts, but then she would picture him undressed beside her, the two of them together with Li'l Pete in the barn loft, in a different reality where no one could ever disturb them. She remembered Li'l Pete's woofs, and Arthur's scent, the pressure from his lips and his thighs, almost too well; they were too real. Was this way of imagining somehow like her mother's fragile mind?

Toward dawn, Meg woke up suddenly and realized she must have finally nodded off. She'd dreamt Arthur was standing in her room, without his clothes, without even his shoes. Yet this hadn't made her restless the way her waking dreams had. And she hadn't worried that Gram or Gramps might walk in while he'd stood there and watched her sleep. Yet she felt as though he'd really been there.

A misty snowfall continued through the morning. On any other Christmas she would have bounded out of bed early. But not this morning. She knew it was time to talk openly with Gram and Gramps about Arthur and

Li'l Pete, and Al and Hank. And she knew her own thoughts would be mirrored in Gram's eyes; she knew Gram's feelings about such things. But it wasn't till she heard voices coming from the living room that she finally lowered her feet onto the floor, her flannel robe chilly against her pajamas. She smoothed her hair quickly as she moved toward the bedroom door, alert to an uncanny feeling that Arthur had actually been there, standing by the door in her dream while she slept.

"Oh, hiya, Viv, June." Meg closed her robe tighter, surprised to see her sisters seated on the sofa, as they rarely visited the flat, even on holidays. "Merry Christmas."

Viv stood so abruptly that the plate of cookies she was holding tilted. June grabbed it before the cookies tipped onto the floor.

"Come in, Meg." Gram frowned from her rocker as Viv slowly sat down again on the sofa.

Meg guessed Gram couldn't mask her chagrin at Viv and June catching Meg having slept so late. Viv would call that laziness. But Gramps frowned, too, which seemed odd on Christmas Day. Then Meg noticed a dull train whistle from the other side of the lake, and right away she wondered what made her notice it.

"Sit down, honey," Gram told her, motioning to a space on the sofa between her sisters.

"We have some news," Viv said quietly. She glanced sideways at Meg, her fingers pressing the hem of her woolen coat. "Bad news. We got word. Ron's been found, Meg. He's in a French hospital. But he's very sick."

Meg's chest clenched inside. *How sick? Yesterday*

he was just missing, wasn't he? Her eyes stung. *At least he's alive! How sick?* The best brother in the world, her one true ally in the family besides Gram. She pictured his dark mop of hair, his square white teeth, his wide hands pitching balls to her during their baseball days. He'd taught her to run properly, less like a girl. His sit-down talks about Mom, her strangeness, how it wasn't anybody's fault, certainly not Meg's, even though Mom got sick right after Meg was born. "It's just one of those things, Megsy," he'd always say. "You're better off with Gram and Gramps." He'd said it many times. "Look how much smarter you got than any of us. Staying over the saloon's not so bad," he'd said.

Viv had waited quietly, her face flushed, holding back her own tears. "Sorry to tell you like this. We got the telegram a few days ago. But when we'd see you catching the bus, we thought we should wait to tell you."

Meg could feel Gram's eyes on her and hear the weak apology in Viv's voice, but she didn't really see or hear anything, or care. Except that Ron's feet had frozen in a trench in France near the Belgium border. Ron, who loved to skate, whose feet always sweat so much. Now he would never wear the socks she'd sent him. She'd knit two pairs, one black, one army green. She'd pictured him putting them on his wide bony feet.

"By the time he got to a hospital," Viv said, "the gangrene was so bad, they had to amputate. Then he caught pneumonia. He's been running a high fever."

All Meg could really think about was Ron's feet. Had they turned blue? Black? What did frozen feet feel like? Had he been in pain, or did they just go numb? Did he suffer when they took them off? What was it

147

like not having any feet? Poor Ronny. She knew a prayer was as useless as the socks she'd sent. And anyway, how many German sisters and mothers were praying, too? How could God possibly choose which side to help in a war? Ron in a French hospital, an amputee with pneumonia—were they taking good care of him? He'd failed French in high school. How would his nurse know if he needed something?

When her thoughts came back to her surroundings, Meg saw Gram's teary eyes from across the room. *Will he live, Gram?* Meg wanted to ask, but her voice wouldn't catch.

"Daddy wanted to come over too, to tell you," Viv said, "but Mom's shook up. He's sitting with her. They didn't sleep much last night. Mom may have to go back to the ward."

Meg put her arm around Viv. Viv, who acted like the mother their Mom could have been if she hadn't been—what? Just too sensitive for life? If only the war hadn't happened—

June shifted closer to Meg from the other end of the sofa. Together the family sat, June, Viv, and Meg staring at the floor, their arms around each other. Gram watching Meg, her rocker making a soft rhythmic moan. Gramps watching out the winter window, frowning back his tears as he petted the cat in his lap.

Chapter 19

Meg spent the day hunched in the chair next to her bedroom window, watching the gray fields and lake without a flurry or breath of snow or wind. Her tears flowed, but she felt empty inside. She stared at the snowy field flecked with bits of cornstalks shorn low to the ground, at the random crow that swooped, cawed, and disappeared into the black branches of a tree. She thought she heard the crackle of wood in the stove from the kitchen, but maybe she imagined it. Eventually she heard low music on the radio, Christmas songs, mostly. She curled her legs tighter against her in the chair, leaned into the wall and the window, and wrestled the day to her, holding onto it before more time had grown between the present moment and the time her sisters told her, before the dim light shifted to darker grays and finally to a faint purple. She watched the purple dissolve to black, till the moon brought back another version of the landscape, otherworldly, barely visible.

****

"You're looking like Jessie Mae was when she was poorly," Greta told Meg on the bus to school one February morning. "We never see you anymore. You're so quiet."

Meg watched a band of slush slide down the bus window. Greta meant well, sure, but it didn't help to talk. Every day was an endless kind of vigil, waiting for news about Ron that never arrived. And Arthur never wrote. She had known he wouldn't, but still she'd hoped—

In English class Mr. B called on her three times, but Meg only shrugged because she hadn't been listening. Of course she'd forced herself to finish *Gatsby*, but she had nothing to say about Daisy and her shallow life. What did a girl like Daisy know about the fear of losing a favorite brother to a war? Meg didn't even blush when Mr. B asked to see her after school. She didn't care. When the three o'clock bell rang, Greta reminded her to stop by Mr. B's room.

"You forgot, didn't you? Aw, Meg." Greta reached out to hug her, but Meg shook herself free, not aggressively, though Greta's eyes teared up. Greta whispered, "I'll see ya," and she walked away, down the corridor, her heels clicking quickly on the scuffed wooden floor. But Meg didn't care, even though she knew she should.

Mr. B was waiting, seated at his desk. "Come in, Meg. Come in."

Meg dropped her books on a desk just inside the room, a little too loudly, and leaned against the door jamb. "I'm sorry about today," she said.

"So am I." Mr. B pushed his glasses down and peered over them at her. "I wish I could say something that would help. But I can't think of anything."

Meg felt her nose burn and the tingle of tears trying to begin. But she was sick of crying. What good was it? No amount of crying could help Ron, or any of the other boys so far from home. If Ron were well enough, he would surely write. And then there was Arthur, who wasn't the kind to write. But she understood. "I never could spell right or read good," he'd always said. He could be anywhere in Germany or France or England, alive, hurt—

"Would it help to talk?" Mr. B asked. His cheeks were rosy in the chilly room. He was tapping his pencil eraser on his desk, probably without realizing he was doing it.

Meg shook her head. "I'll pay attention tomorrow. I read the book—"

Mr. B smiled and sighed with what sounded like disappointment. "I'm not concerned about the book," Mr. B said. "I'm concerned about you."

Meg noticed for the first time ever that his irises were surrounded by fuzzy velvet rings of black, just like Sam, Gramps' cat.

"Don't worry," she told him. "I'm fine." Turning to leave, she picked up her books. "And thanks."

"If you feel like talking," Mr. B said, "I'm here."

She nodded and left the room, walking as fast as she could to breathe the cold outside air, to feel wind sting her cheeks, falling snow touch her hair. She plodded along on snow-padded sidewalks to Chef's, where taking orders, carrying plates, adding bills, and making change at the register kept her mind busy for a few hours.

Chapter 20

One evening when Meg returned home from her afternoon shift at Chef's, Charley was standing oddly behind the bar in the dim saloon. Just to his left, a figure slouched on one of the stools, a figure too well dressed for a usual customer. From the floor near the bar, Meg heard Brandy panting as if to say hello.

Charley edged toward the back door and clucked to Brandy. "Come on, girl," he said, glancing at Meg with a frown. Brandy's nails skidded on the wooden floor as she trotted for the back door. She woofed, then quickly she and Charley slipped out, leaving the saloon silent.

Meg's stomach knotted as she turned toward the back stairs. Usually Charley was careful not to leave her alone with customers. The figure at the bar was standing. His hand gripped the bar.

"H'lo, Meg."

The familiar voice carried the affectation of an actor or a con man. Meg's eyes had adjusted to the dark saloon, and she recognized the man's suit as an army uniform. Then his blue eyes and chiseled jaw came into focus in the shadows.

"Hank."

"Surprised to see me, I bet."

He smirked, but in a less assured way than she remembered. He even leaned forward as if to step toward her—to give her a kiss? But his hand bumped an empty shot glass. She watched him fumble to set it right again. He glanced at her just at that moment, as if to see if she'd noticed. His smirk returned, and he sat back on the stool.

"You got prettier. More grown up." He rubbed his jaw with the back of his wrist. "Things sure change, don't they?"

She recalled how the whites of his eyes used to be clear as snow. Now they were dull and bloodshot like a circus clown's. His golden skin was cherry pink in places, or ashen. Stray whiskers spotted his neck and chin. When she looked into his eyes, he squinted.

"Just dropped in for a quick one with Charley," he blurted, running his fingers through unwashed hair. He crossed his legs. "I'd've cleaned up better if I'd known I'd be seeing you. Got my letters, didn't you?"

"Yes. Thank you." She moved closer till she could smell cigarette smoke in his clothes. She remembered how he wore cologne before he left for the war. She wondered if he knew about Li'l Pete and Al and Arthur. "Did you get the letters I sent you?" she asked.

"Sure. And my mom's. You two were my stars. I never slept over there, so I read your letters a hundred times a night." He balanced a trembling hand on the bar. His nails were ragged. "Crazy, isn't it? You had another life with me, in my head. And you never knew."

She placed her hand gently on the bar. This was Hank, a soldier come home. She imagined this could be her brother Ron. "When did you get back?"

"Oh, I dunno. Kind of lost track." His eyes traced the outline of her hair. "So what's this I hear about you and Arthur?"

She glanced down to see his fingers stretch toward hers. Without thinking, she withdrew her hand from the bar. Her face flushed.

"Don't you know that's a train going nowhere?" He chuckled. "Guy like that, he won't ever finish high school. He's not for you."

Inside she shouted, *You don't know what you're talking about—Arthur's better than any of you—And it was most likely Al who killed our puppy—or one of his friends!* But she didn't. She kept her voice steady. "Let's not talk about that right now."

His eyes quivered; then he looked away, at a corner of the room. He seemed suddenly confused. She could see dark stains inside his collar, where a vein in his neck pulsed, protruded. This tired man bore no resemblance to the Hank Wickham she'd known all her life.

"It's good to see you, Hank. Welcome home."

She touched his arm gently, but he knocked her away, grazing her chin sharply with his fist. She cried out, more from surprise than hurt. Mostly she felt stunned and held her chin in her hand. Then she noticed tears in his eyes. He stood up abruptly.

"Sorry—" He pulled himself around to behind the bar, then held a shaky hand in the air. "Sorry. Could you give me a minute?"

"Sure. Of course." She wanted to run upstairs. If only Charley would come back. She wished this day had never happened.

With two hands, Hank maneuvered a whiskey bottle to the shot glass, then nodded at Meg. Quickly she understood what he wanted and steadied the glass. After he drank, he poured another shot and drank that too, staring past her into the dim room. His eyes cleared, and he tilted his head.

"Didn't know I'd come back lousy, did you?"

"You're not lousy—" she said.

"Hell." He let out a long breath thick with whiskey and stared past Meg at the corner of the room. "You just don't know."

"You served your country, Hank—"

"Seems simple to you, doesn't it." He laughed. "Just like my mother."

Meg turned to leave, not out of anger as much as an uneasiness. He seemed strange, uncontrolled. "I'd better go upstairs," she mumbled, but he grabbed her elbow. Too rough at first, he softened his grasp.

"Wait," he said. "Don't go yet." His eyes were glassy and sad.

"I have to go, Hank. Stop by another time, all right?" She gently pried his fingers off her arm.

Just then the back door to the saloon creaked open as Charley entered, with Brandy padding behind him.

"Damn cold out there," Charley muttered.

"I better go, Hank." Meg backed away toward the back stairs. "You take care of yourself, all right? Rest."

"Sure thing." He ran his fingers through his hair. "We'll go for a drive soon. Soon as the ice melts."

Chapter 21

The next night when she returned home and entered the saloon, Hank was alert at the bar, with Charley and Brandy nowhere in sight. Meg lowered her head and strode straight for the stairs. Her legs stung from having waded through the snowdrifts that blocked the walk up to the front door. But Hank slid off his stool and intercepted her.

"What's your hurry?" He stretched his arm across the railing, blocking the stairs. "How was work?"

He seemed quite sober in spite of the sweet scent of alcohol on his breath. His hair was still greasy, and his uniform sagged. She watched his eyes focus first on her shoulder and then her shoes before he looked up into her face.

"So how was it?" he asked. The remnant of alcohol might have been a liqueur—anise? The licorice-tasting kind that Charley let her sip secretly on her fifteenth birthday?

"Work was just fine." She kept her voice steady, casual. Her damp legs made her shiver a little, and she absentmindedly twisted Arthur's bracelet around her wrist. "But I'm real tired. And I've got school tomorrow. Homework, too."

Hank chuckled and leaned forward a little. "Smart girl still. Well, good for you." Then he pulled his arm away from the rail and stepped back. "Keep it up.

156

That's swell. Being smart can take you places."

She felt she should give him a word of encouragement. *You, too, Hank. You were always one of the smartest. Everybody said so.* But she didn't. Why couldn't Ron and Arthur be standing there, instead of Hank? A wicked thought, she knew, but there it was.

Hank smiled at her sadly, then leaned forward again and whispered, "Me, I can't remember anything half the time." He looked as if he might cry, but he laughed instead. "Dumb like Al now. Can't concentrate or anything."

He had that faraway, vacant stare her mother had so much of the time. "But don't you worry," he told her. "I'll be all right."

Without thinking, she shook his arm, gripping his sleeve as if to wake him up.

"What's wrong, Hank? What's happening with you?" She felt guilty, sorry for her impatience with him, her disgust, really. Then his eyes seemed to focus on her clearly for the first time since he'd been back.

"You don't need to hear those kinds of things," he said.

"What kind?" She took hold of his sleeve again and shook it, more gently this time.

His eyes were wet, not with tears exactly, but wet, as if they would turn into tears if he weren't so determined not to let them.

"They don't like us sharing those things," he said.

"What things? Who's they?"

"It's my problem," he said. "I just got to deal with it."

"What?" she said, still holding onto his sleeve. Maybe she didn't want to hear it. Maybe it was better kept inside him. But then again, maybe it would help to tell somebody.

"Haven't you told anybody?" she asked. He shook his head no. Then he shook his arm free and stepped back a step, but he leaned his head toward her. He was staring at her boots.

"We'd been living in the snow for weeks," he said. "Guys' toes were freezing, rotting, see. We got caught, and the Krauts rounded us up like livestock. At some place where the roads meet, at the Belgium border, they pretended we were prisoners, but it was more like a firing squad. Somebody broke rank, or they fired a shot, I'm not sure which. I started to run—"

"Anybody would," she said.

"No," he snapped, addressing the corner of the room. "We had orders to stay in line. But I didn't. I couldn't. My buddy's head exploded on me when we ran. His brains got in my hair. Pink bits. Some days I smell 'em."

He stepped away, then walked out the back of the saloon without his coat. It was draped over one of the stools at the bar. Meg thought maybe he was just off to pee in the snow, that he'd be back in a minute, but minutes passed. She thought to run after him with it but stood still at the stairs instead. A kind of inertia held her like thick cotton ropes. Even when Charley came in the back door with Brandy, Meg stood at the banister, staring after Hank, feeling a phantom trace of something, something she wouldn't be able to shake away.

"Get to bed, missy," Charley said. "Hurry upstairs before he comes back in. Ain't you got school tomorrow?"

She faced upstairs and dragged her legs up each step.

Chapter 22

Upstairs, on her bed waiting for her, was a letter from Ron, written in a feminine cursive, very likely by his French nurse.

Megsi, Well I made it. May be not all of me made it, but most of me did. Gess there wont be anymore skating on Seneca for this old soldier, but hell. It will be good to come home. The nerses here are the best. Sure do wish I had payed more attention to French classe. Give my love to Gram and Gramps. Keep up your studys. With some bonne chance (thats French for good luck!), I will be there for your graduation. Love, Ron.

She read the letter again and again, finally slipping under her covers, still dressed in her waitress uniform, hugging the letter to her till she fell asleep.

Next morning, a loud thud woke Meg up. Then a group of crows cried. She looked out her window and saw that a heavy branch had fallen off an old oak tree. A ragged halo of icicles dimpled the new snow surrounding the branch. Wind gusted, sending flurries in all directions like confetti. Meg tucked Ron's letter into a drawer and reached into her dresser for her skating clothes, pulling Gram's old woolens and snowpants on over her uniform. She picked up her boots and tiptoed down the hall, so as not to wake her grandparents, and slipped out of the flat and down the stairs into the dim saloon.

Hank was slumped on a stool, asleep, snoring quietly, his head and chest resting on the bar. Meg made her way noiselessly across the wooden floor to the front door, where she put on her boots. Leaning against the wall was Charley's snow shovel. She lifted it slowly, quietly, pulling on her hat and mittens, and opening the door with barely a sound. Once outside, she began to shovel the front stoop in the frozen early morning darkness.

The wind had been blowing off the lake from the west, so the air around the saloon stoop was sheltered and still. Meg dug shallow shovelfuls, careful not to scrape concrete. She loved the privacy of the dark, early morning. She could think about Arthur and Ron uninterrupted. She could miss them, even talk to them, and imagine them at home, asleep in their beds here in Valois.

Even though the snow was light and easy to lift, her back and arms worked hard. She heard Ron's words in her head, "I will be there for your graduation." She worked harder, remembering how he'd taught her to bend her knees, lift with her legs, not her back. She tossed rhythmic shovelfuls over her shoulder, leaving dents in the unblemished snow. Every shovelful worked her legs, arms, even her stomach, and she began to feel too warm under her coat. Soon she had begun to sweat. Her raw cheeks alone felt the biting chill.

As she advanced her way down the walk toward the highway, gusts of wind found their way around the shield of the saloon. A glow from beyond her parents' house lightened the morning from the east. She glanced toward the cemetery and then heard in her own shovelfuls the sound of Arthur's shovel covering Li'l

Pete's grave. Today it seemed as if all of Valois was a memorial honoring the fighting men, with the living walking around like caretakers for the plots of those who were gone—the longtime local families like the Lees, the Civil War soldiers buried high in the cemetery, the ancient Senecas buried higher up the hill where Li'l Pete lay. Even, in a way, Meg's mom, stuck in her purgatory state of suspended life, someone who'd given up long ago. And then there was Hank, a haunted warrior back among the living.

By the time Meg reached the end of the walk, the snow had become heavier where the snowplow had left behind a mound. She dug harder and threw heavier shovelfuls with shorter sweeps. When she turned back to survey her work, she saw that Hank was standing in the open doorway of the saloon in his calf-length army coat, watching her. As soon as she had turned, he stepped down onto the stoop, closing the door gently behind him.

"Nice work," he voiced with just enough volume for her to hear, tilting his head to the side.

She felt a rush of something—*Shame on him for wasting his time in the saloon every day with Ron injured and Arthur off somewhere, anywhere.* Hank was safe here at home. He could eat hot meals, get hot showers, never ever have to fire again at a fellow soldier. Hank's limbs were intact. He was walking around freely on two good feet.

"Here," she said, rushing over to him, thrusting the shovel into his hands. "Everyone needs their walk done. Go on." She spun around behind him and herded him down the walk, her arm across his back, pushing against his shoulders.

Hank paused at the edge of the highway, holding the shovel upright. He blinked at her, his jaw lax, appearing caught between annoyance and disbelief. Or maybe it was just that he was still waking up.

"Go on," she urged, desperate, her hands flapping like Aunt Lizzie shooing chickens. "Go, Hank. Why not? Go!"

He stepped away from her, frowning, and started down along the edge of the highway toward the Lees' house. Perhaps it was the shame of seeing a girl shovel snow. But he set the shovel over his shoulder like a rifle and didn't look back.

Chapter 23

She set off down the hill for the lake shore. A gust of gray swirled around her and seagulls flew overhead, their caws like shouts. She felt that the spirits of loved ones were waiting for her, not up in the cemetery, but down the hill at the lake. Aunt May would be there, she could feel it. And Li'l Pete. And some of the local boys who weren't coming home from the war. If she dallied, she felt she'd miss them, so she charged down the unplowed road with an extra reserve of breath, her boots heavy on the crunchy snow. The brittle air didn't sting her throat. It was a steady run.

Winds had dusted the snow from the western side of the trees that lined the lake. Their stark black limbs bent with grace to the sharp wind. Waves rolled ocean-like in teams of diagonals, crashed on the shore, then tumbled under themselves to make way for the next group. The navy blue surface of the water interlaced with black and silver as the morning gradually brightened. Meg edged down to the rim of the shore, no longer frozen. The snow had dissolved onto wet shale stones and shells; there she listened. She knelt and even while freezing drafts of lake air brushed her face and hair, she felt warm enough from the run. Her snowpants kept her knees dry.

Within the din of waves and wind, Meg heard the faint sound of a cardinal's song from his perch in a pine nearby on shore. She scanned the trees and spotted his red body jostling in a low bough, disturbing the female gripping the branch close to him, her gray body almost invisible except for red streaks in her wings and tail. The male's song changed pitch. Its quick, rhythmic melody added life to the wild, noisy air.

Meg whispered out loud, "Arthur?"

She remembered a story he had told her the one time she asked him how his father died.

"My grandma tells this," Arthur'd said. "White folks don't like it much."

She could hear Arthur now inside her head, his voice mixing with the cardinal's song.

"At first, there wasn't any such thing as death," Arthur had said. "Until there were so many people on earth that it got too crowded. The chiefs held a council, and somebody said maybe people should go away for a little while when they died, to make more room, and then come back later.

"But Coyote said folks should die forever because otherwise people would run out of food. Folks didn't want to lose their family and friends, though, because they'd feel too sad and lose all the happiness in their hearts.

"So the medicine man built a grass house where he would sing a song to call the spirits of the dead back to life. And when the first man died, the medicine man sang. Ten days later a strong wind blew and circled the grass house. But Coyote had shut the door, so the spirit whirled past, because it found the door to the grass house closed.

"So now spirits of the dead wander like gusts of wind, looking for the road to the spirit land."

As Meg watched, the cardinal and his mate shifted and quickly took flight, disappearing into the woods above the shore, leaving the choir of waves to the shouting gulls.

What if Ron came back from the war like Hank, or worse, bitter or even cruel? So what if it wasn't in his nature; war changed people. Sure, he would have to use a wheelchair now. Or maybe he could get prosthetic feet and be able to use crutches. Whatever happened, he would adjust somehow. She felt sure of it. He would find a way.

She felt the urge to see her mother, to tell her maybe Ron's accident had spared him something, that at least now he wouldn't have to kill German soldiers and he was out of harm's way. But talking to her mother never seemed to help. She could say the same things to Gram, and Gram would understand. Maybe her mother was beyond reach, ever. Maybe it was time to let that go. To stop wishing for something that would never be.

The wind in her eyes sent tears down Meg's cheeks, but she wasn't crying. Yet she felt the same kind of release. She knew the sun must be rising behind her because the waves shone with white and yellow stripes, and the sky above the far shore grew lighter. The wind quieted, and the waves gradually slowed and lost their force. Meg smiled slowly at the change, as if the lake had performed its magic just for her.

"Arthur, come home," she whispered.

A gull cried from down the shore, then took off and flew south toward Watkins. It was most likely time to head to school. She hoped she hadn't missed her bus.

Chapter 24

By late spring, Seneca's hillsides were in full bloom. With warmer, dryer weather, folks rediscovered neighbors they hadn't seen for months, sharing news of loved ones and renewed hope for their safe returns.

Meg wrote to Arthur almost daily, telling him everything that had happened since he'd left, leaving out details she guessed the censors might object to. Even though she hadn't heard from him, even though she wasn't sure he'd receive her V-mails, she trusted that somehow just writing him would help. She told him about Cornell, how she'd applied and been accepted, and how her New York State scholarship would cover her tuition. She wasn't exactly sure how she'd find money to live on, but life was to live, as Gram would say, so she just believed that she would find a way.

Then, early on the morning of May 8th, Meg woke to Gramps pounding on her bedroom door shouting, "Them Krauts surrendered, Meg!" Victory in Europe Day had arrived. The Germans had surrendered unconditionally. Hitler was dead. Now, maybe, finally, Arthur would come home.

At school that day, and later at work, the people of Watkins Glen celebrated. Meg sped through her tasks with aplomb, smiling, remembering orders, but all the while wishing she had heard from Arthur.

Why can't he write? Just once? Please bring him home safe.

Then, when she arrived home that evening of V-E Day, Gram's smile and nod toward her bedroom told her perhaps, just perhaps, at last—

The V-mail lay on her bed. Meg closed her door and turned on her lamp. Gently she broke the seal and waited. The moon out her open window shone full over the western shore. The scent of forsythia and lilac wafted into her room. Down the hill, a lone gull cried. She opened the flap and spread the page on her bedcover, revealing carefully blocked letters written in black ink.

Hello Meg. Thank you for your letters. I wish I rote as good as you. Please know I think of you evry day and night. Soon we will come home and I will get to see you. I am a Timberwolf. Wish I had good news to tell but life hear is no good. Wurse than you can imagin. We found a camp Dora with prisoners so starved. They looked like childrens skeletins with skin for cloths. We fed them pig soup. Then we rounded up the Germans who live close by. We made them bury the dead. To show them what happened. It dont make no sence. What was all the killing and hate for? I will tell you more when I come home. Be well. Love, Arthur.

****

Come June, the morning of Watkins Glen High School's graduation, everyone gathered at Lakeside Park at the southern tip of Seneca Lake. The day brought the best of blustery early summer with the sun refracting off the lake. From her seat on the outdoor stage, Meg scanned the rows of expectant faces, many wearing dark sunglasses or shielding their eyes with their hands in a kind of salute. She spotted Hank and Charley seated in the back, in the same row as her parents and sisters. She could see her mother's face, expressionless as always, but Meg guessed that deep inside her mom was proud. Then Gramps waved to Meg from the front row, where he had staked out his claim very early that morning.

"We can't hear if we set in back," he'd practically shouted. "We want to hear that valedict'ry speech again. It's a good 'un."

Meg had practiced her speech in the kitchen to that biased and favorable audience, Gramps with his smiles and nods, and Gram, who mouthed along with some of the words, offering suggestions. "Keep your chin up, honey. Let us see your face... Couldn't hear that last word. Speak up. Be sure to smile."

Next to Meg's grandparents in the front row sat Mr. and Mrs. Lee, alongside Arthur's grandma in her broad-brimmed straw hat, flowered dress, and embroidered moccasins. And best of all, at the end of the row sat Ron, dressed in his full uniform, wearing sunglasses, seated tall in his wheelchair.

When Mr. B called Meg up to the podium that morning in June, Meg looked to Ron, who tipped his sunglasses down and shot her a wink. She smiled back at him and put her hand to her heart, then looked to Greta, who was seated beside her. They squeezed hands just as the breeze from the lake flipped the tassels on their flat board hats, which made them giggle. They'd been little girls together, and now they were both bound for Ithaca, or "over the hill" as it was known in Valois.

In that frantic instant before she spoke, Meg imagined Arthur was there, too. She would mention him in her speech, for his grandma's sake and the sake of all the families whose men were heroes now. She imagined Li'l Pete romping with Arthur in the background. If he could have been there, Arthur would surely have sat next to Ron and would have worn his uniform too. He no doubt had military hair now, cut unrecognizably short. She jingled his bracelet out from beneath the sleeve of her black gown and patted his letter that lay in the pocket of her shirtwaist. It was then she decided to change her speech. Not a lot. Just a bit. Just enough.

Maybe war isn't the answer. Could she say this? Could her generation find a way to stop fighting wars?

She took a breath at the podium, and recognized that this was farewell, that it was time to leave Valois. Her sisters might never leave home. Gramps and Gram would always be there. Most likely Ron, and Hank, and Charley, too. But it was time for her to move on. This was her chance to say good-bye and tell them why. She took a second breath, then began.

A word about the author…

Raised in Buffalo, NY, summering on Seneca Lake among her parents' extended families, Emily followed her mother's path to Cornell University. She was inspired by the Finger Lakes' fertile history as birthplace of the women's movement, as the spot where Twain imagined Huckleberry Finn, as a stopping point along the Underground Railroad.

At Cornell she majored in English. A lifelong diarist and avid reader, with a mother who provided summer reading lists to her and her two sisters, Emily dreamed of writing professionally. But an acting class at Cornell, taught by a future Pulitzer Prize winner, bit her with the acting bug. She went on to stand-by on Broadway, appear in television commercials, and act with major regional companies including Berkeley Repertory, Actors Theatre of Louisville, and A Noise Within. What a joy to speak the words of great playwrights, from Shakespeare to Shaw, from Larry Shue to Sarah Ruhl!

Then, as a mom and Theatre Arts professor, she rediscovered her first love, writing. She published with *The Christian Science Monitor* and wrote documentary scripts for special features on such DVDs as *The Hours*, *Tuck Everlasting*, and *The Passion*.

Currently she and her film professor husband teach at Chapman University, spending summers at their mountain home with their adopted dog and two cats.

Seneca Lake is her first novel.

https://www.emilyheebner.com